A LUCKY LUKE ADVENTURE

THE DALTONS IN THE BLIZZARD

BY MORRIS & GOSCINNY

9th CINEBOOK
The 9th Art Publisher

Original title: Lucky Luke – Les Dalton dans le Blizzard

Original edition: © Dargaud Editeur Paris 1971 by Goscinny and Morris
© Lucky Comics
www.lucky-luke.com

English translation: © 2008 Cinebook Ltd

Translator: Luke Spear
Lettering and text layout: Imadjinn sarl

This edition first published in Great Britain in 2009 by
Cinebook Ltd
56 Beech Avenue
Canterbury, Kent
CT4 7TA
www.cinebook.com

Second printing: February 2014
Printed in Spain by Just Colour Graphic

A CIP catalogue record for this book
is available from the British Library

ISBN 978-1-905460-76-2

9th CINEBOOK
The 9th Art Publisher

THE DALTONS IN THE BLIZZARD

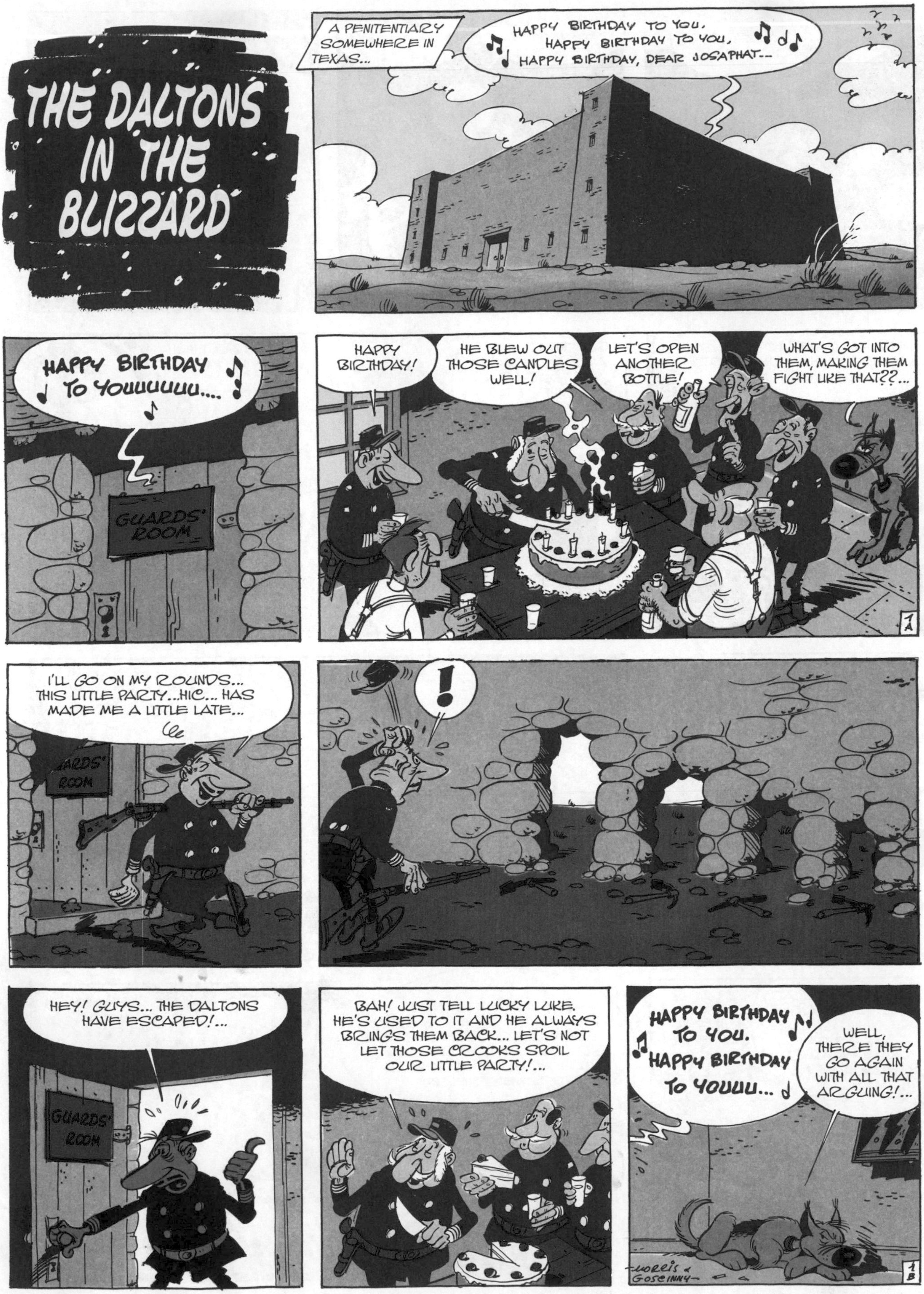
A PENITENTIARY SOMEWHERE IN TEXAS...
HAPPY BIRTHDAY TO YOU, HAPPY BIRTHDAY TO YOU, HAPPY BIRTHDAY, DEAR JOSAPHAT--
HAPPY BIRTHDAY TO YOUUUUUU....
GUARDS' ROOM
HAPPY BIRTHDAY!
HE BLEW OUT THOSE CANDLES WELL!
LET'S OPEN ANOTHER BOTTLE!
WHAT'S GOT INTO THEM, MAKING THEM FIGHT LIKE THAT??...
I'LL GO ON MY ROUNDS... THIS LITTLE PARTY...HIC... HAS MADE ME A LITTLE LATE...
GUARDS' ROOM
!
HEY! GUYS... THE DALTONS HAVE ESCAPED!...
GUARDS' ROOM
BAH! JUST TELL LUCKY LUKE. HE'S USED TO IT AND HE ALWAYS BRINGS THEM BACK... LET'S NOT LET THOSE CROOKS SPOIL OUR LITTLE PARTY!...
HAPPY BIRTHDAY TO YOU. HAPPY BIRTHDAY TO YOUUU...
WELL, THERE THEY GO AGAIN WITH ALL THAT ARGUING!...
MORRIS & GOSCINNY

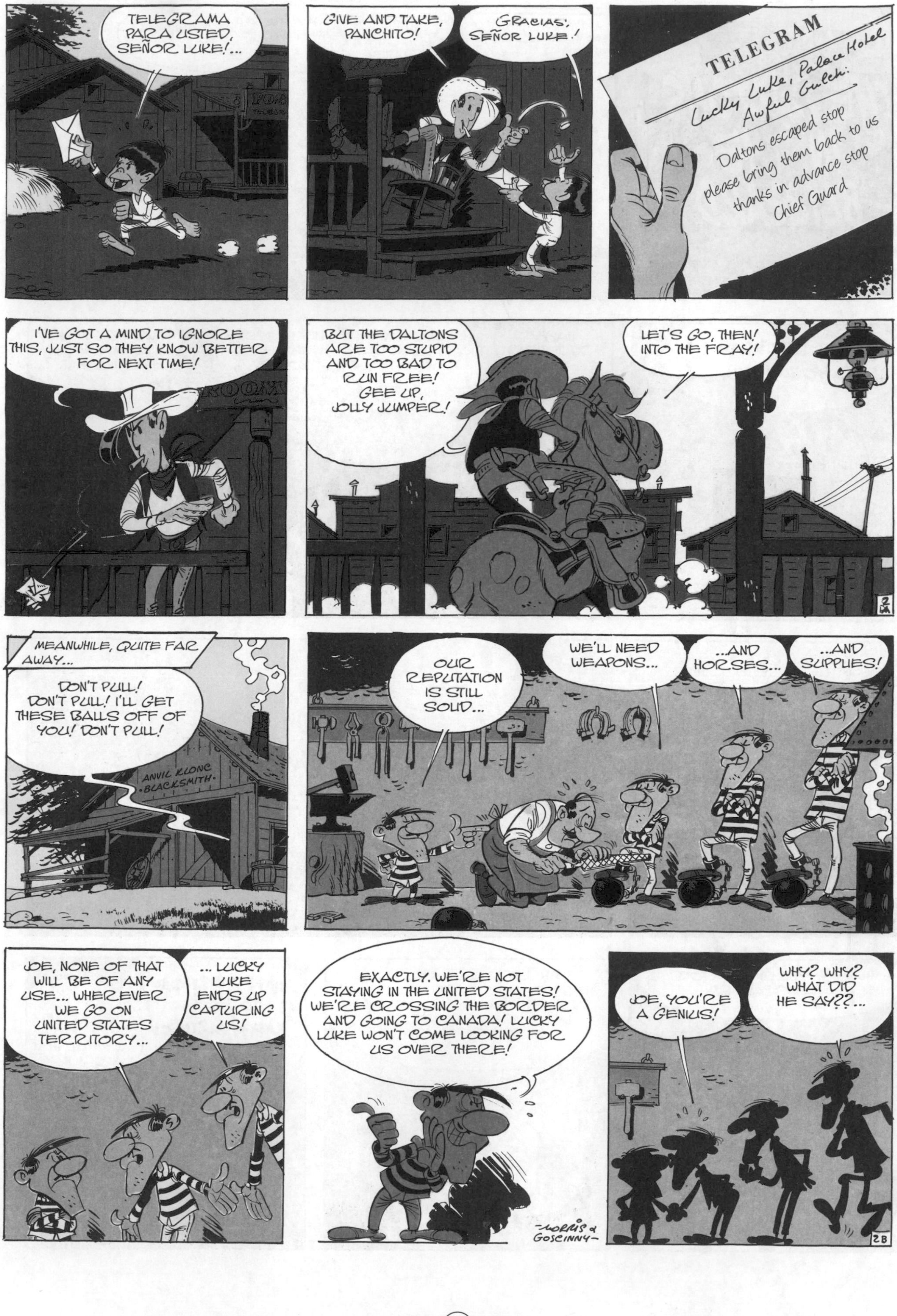
TELEGRAMA PARA USTED, SEÑOR LUKE!...
GIVE AND TAKE, PANCHITO!
GRACIAS, SEÑOR LUKE!
TELEGRAM
Lucky Luke, Palace Hotel Awful Gulch.
Daltons escaped stop please bring them back to us thanks in advance stop Chief Guard
I'VE GOT A MIND TO IGNORE THIS, JUST SO THEY KNOW BETTER FOR NEXT TIME!
BUT THE DALTONS ARE TOO STUPID AND TOO BAD TO RUN FREE! GEE UP, JOLLY JUMPER!
LET'S GO, THEN! INTO THE FRAY!
MEANWHILE, QUITE FAR AWAY...
DON'T PULL! DON'T PULL! I'LL GET THESE BALLS OFF OF YOU! DON'T PULL!
ANVIL KLONC BLACKSMITH
OUR REPUTATION IS STILL SOLID...
WE'LL NEED WEAPONS...
...AND HORSES...
...AND SUPPLIES!
JOE, NONE OF THAT WILL BE OF ANY USE... WHEREVER WE GO ON UNITED STATES TERRITORY...
... LUCKY LUKE ENDS UP CAPTURING US!
EXACTLY. WE'RE NOT STAYING IN THE UNITED STATES! WE'RE CROSSING THE BORDER AND GOING TO CANADA! LUCKY LUKE WON'T COME LOOKING FOR US OVER THERE!
MORRIS & GOSCINNY
JOE, YOU'RE A GENIUS!
WHY? WHY? WHAT DID HE SAY??...

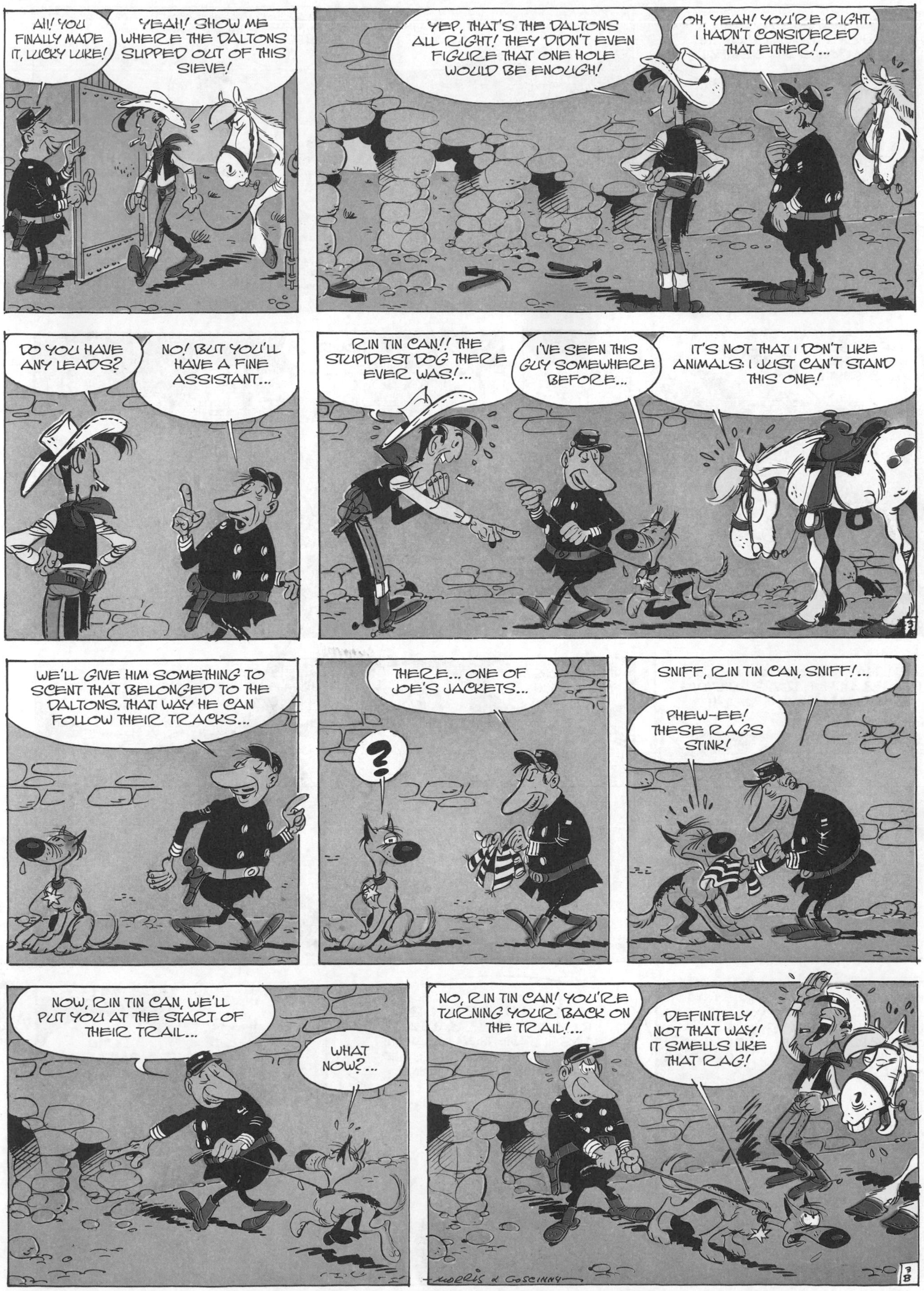
AH! YOU FINALLY MADE IT, LUCKY LUKE!
YEAH! SHOW ME WHERE THE DALTONS SLIPPED OUT OF THIS SIEVE!
YEP, THAT'S THE DALTONS ALL RIGHT! THEY DIDN'T EVEN FIGURE THAT ONE HOLE WOULD BE ENOUGH!
OH, YEAH! YOU'RE RIGHT. I HADN'T CONSIDERED THAT EITHER!...
DO YOU HAVE ANY LEADS?
NO! BUT YOU'LL HAVE A FINE ASSISTANT...
RIN TIN CAN!! THE STUPIDEST DOG THERE EVER WAS!...
I'VE SEEN THIS GUY SOMEWHERE BEFORE...
IT'S NOT THAT I DON'T LIKE ANIMALS: I JUST CAN'T STAND THIS ONE!
WE'LL GIVE HIM SOMETHING TO SCENT THAT BELONGED TO THE DALTONS. THAT WAY HE CAN FOLLOW THEIR TRACKS...
?
THERE... ONE OF JOE'S JACKETS...
SNIFF, RIN TIN CAN, SNIFF!...
PHEW-EE! THESE RAGS STINK!
NOW, RIN TIN CAN, WE'LL PUT YOU AT THE START OF THEIR TRAIL...
WHAT NOW?...
NO, RIN TIN CAN! YOU'RE TURNING YOUR BACK ON THE TRAIL!...
DEFINITELY NOT THAT WAY! IT SMELLS LIKE THAT RAG!
MORRIS & GOSCINNY

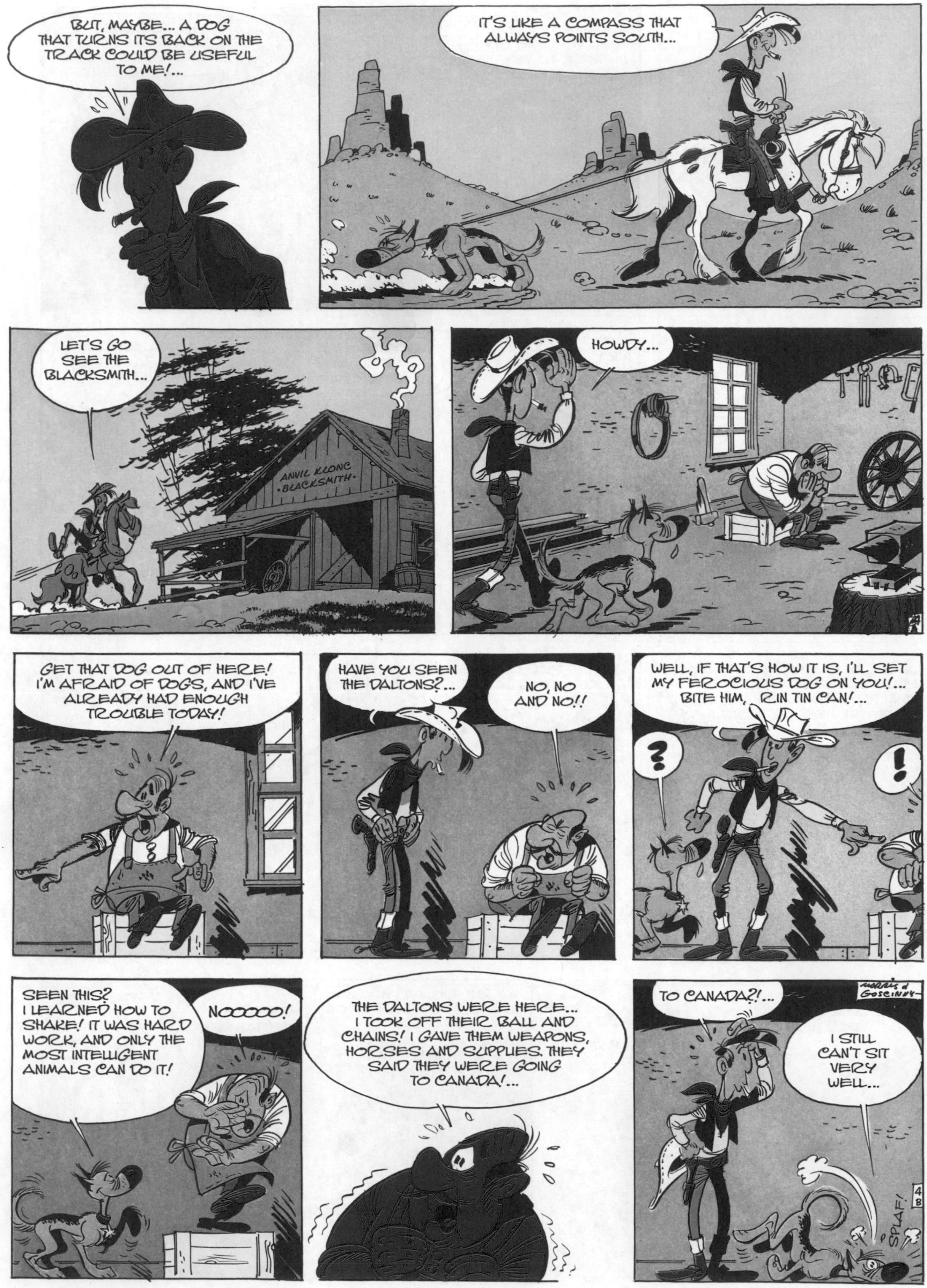
BUT, MAYBE... A DOG THAT TURNS ITS BACK ON THE TRACK COULD BE USEFUL TO ME!...
IT'S LIKE A COMPASS THAT ALWAYS POINTS SOUTH...
LET'S GO SEE THE BLACKSMITH...
ANVIL KLONC BLACKSMITH
HOWDY...
GET THAT DOG OUT OF HERE! I'M AFRAID OF DOGS, AND I'VE ALREADY HAD ENOUGH TROUBLE TODAY!
HAVE YOU SEEN THE DALTONS?...
NO, NO AND NO!!
WELL, IF THAT'S HOW IT IS, I'LL SET MY FEROCIOUS DOG ON YOU!... BITE HIM, RIN TIN CAN!...
?
!
SEEN THIS? I LEARNED HOW TO SHAKE! IT WAS HARD WORK, AND ONLY THE MOST INTELLIGENT ANIMALS CAN DO IT!
NOOOOOO!
THE DALTONS WERE HERE... I TOOK OFF THEIR BALL AND CHAINS! I GAVE THEM WEAPONS, HORSES AND SUPPLIES. THEY SAID THEY WERE GOING TO CANADA!...
TO CANADA?!...
I STILL CAN'T SIT VERY WELL...
SPLAF!

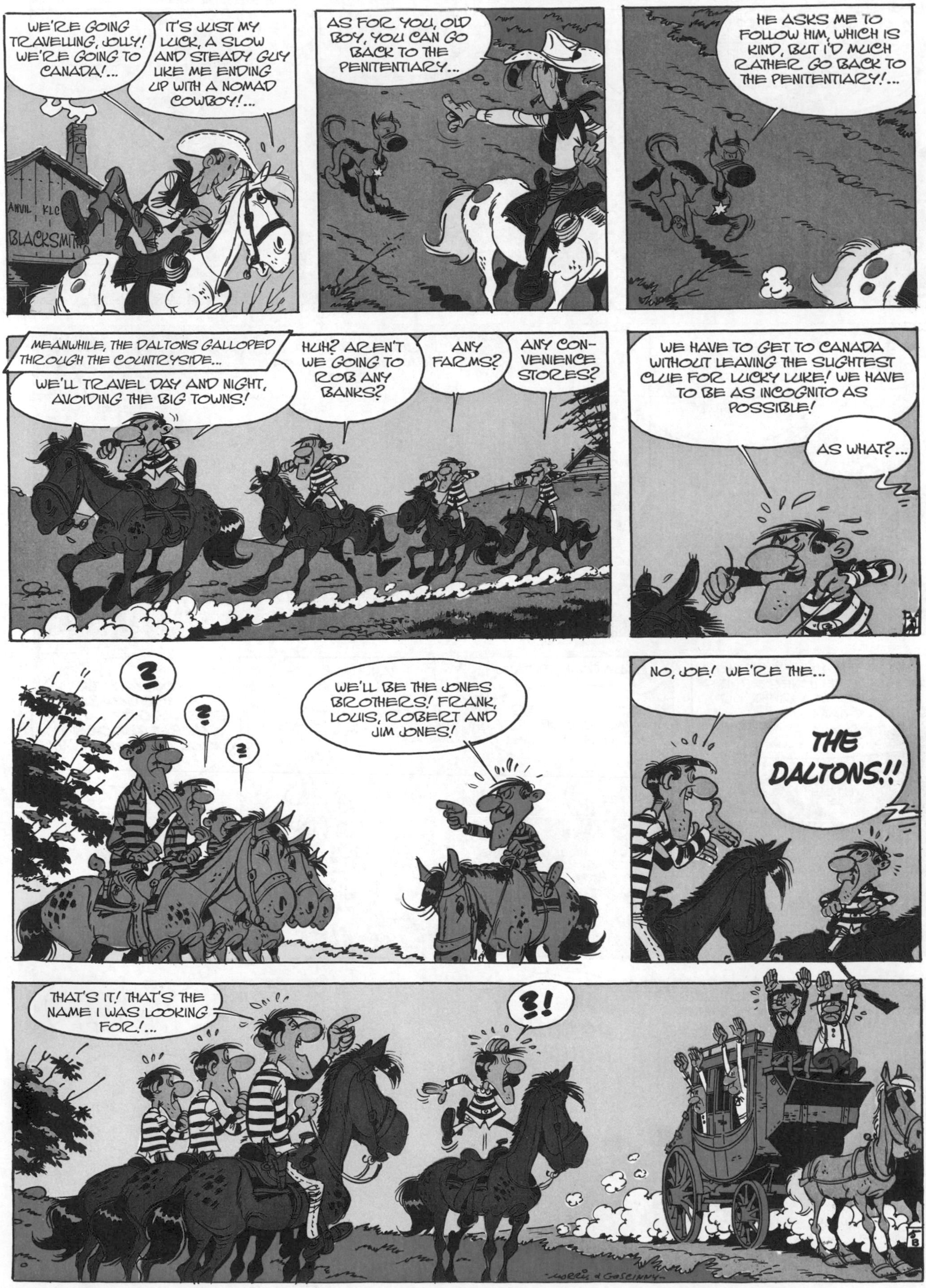

WE'RE GOING TRAVELLING, JOLLY! WE'RE GOING TO CANADA!...
IT'S JUST MY LUCK, A SLOW AND STEADY GUY LIKE ME ENDING UP WITH A NOMAD COWBOY!...
ANVIL KLC
BLACKSMI
AS FOR YOU, OLD BOY, YOU CAN GO BACK TO THE PENITENTIARY...
HE ASKS ME TO FOLLOW HIM, WHICH IS KIND, BUT I'D MUCH RATHER GO BACK TO THE PENITENTIARY!...
MEANWHILE, THE DALTONS GALLOPED THROUGH THE COUNTRYSIDE...
WE'LL TRAVEL DAY AND NIGHT, AVOIDING THE BIG TOWNS!
HUH? AREN'T WE GOING TO ROB ANY BANKS?
ANY FARMS?
ANY CONVENIENCE STORES?
WE HAVE TO GET TO CANADA WITHOUT LEAVING THE SLIGHTEST CLUE FOR LUCKY LUKE! WE HAVE TO BE AS INCOGNITO AS POSSIBLE!
AS WHAT?...
?
?
?
WE'LL BE THE JONES BROTHERS! FRANK, LOUIS, ROBERT AND JIM JONES!
NO, JOE! WE'RE THE...
THE DALTONS!!
THAT'S IT! THAT'S THE NAME I WAS LOOKING FOR!...
?!
MORRIS & GOSCINNY

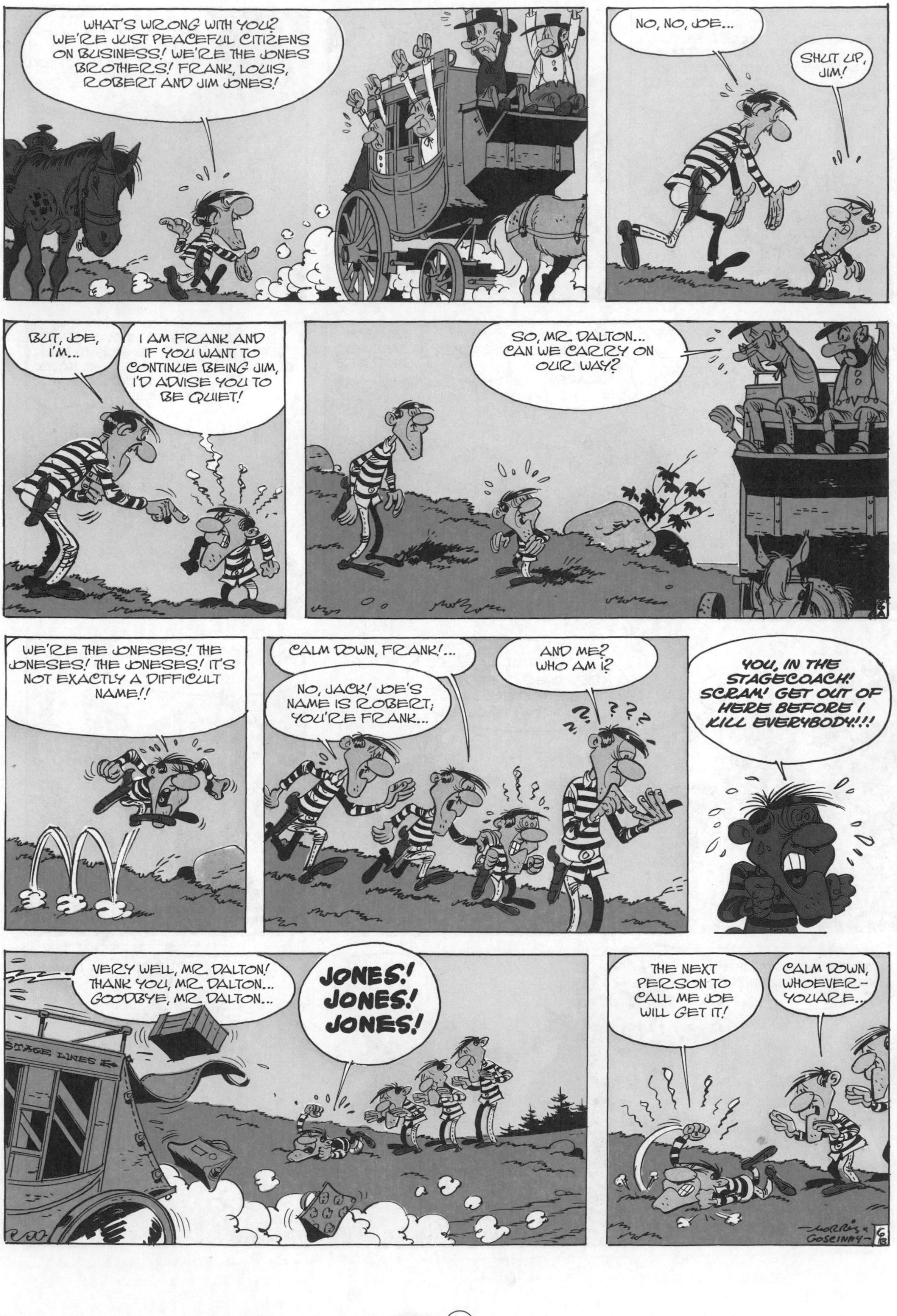
WHAT'S WRONG WITH YOU? WE'RE JUST PEACEFUL CITIZENS ON BUSINESS! WE'RE THE JONES BROTHERS! FRANK, LOUIS, ROBERT AND JIM JONES!
NO, NO, JOE...
SHUT UP, JIM!
BUT, JOE, I'M...
I AM FRANK AND IF YOU WANT TO CONTINUE BEING JIM, I'D ADVISE YOU TO BE QUIET!
SO, MR. DALTON... CAN WE CARRY ON OUR WAY?
WE'RE THE JONESES! THE JONESES! THE JONESES! IT'S NOT EXACTLY A DIFFICULT NAME!!
CALM DOWN, FRANK!...
NO, JACK! JOE'S NAME IS ROBERT; YOU'RE FRANK...
AND ME? WHO AM I?
YOU, IN THE STAGECOACH! SCRAM! GET OUT OF HERE BEFORE I KILL EVERYBODY!!!
VERY WELL, MR. DALTON! THANK YOU, MR. DALTON... GOODBYE, MR. DALTON...
JONES! JONES! JONES!
STAGE LINES
THE NEXT PERSON TO CALL ME JOE WILL GET IT!
CALM DOWN, WHOEVER-YOUARE...
MORRIS GOSCINNY

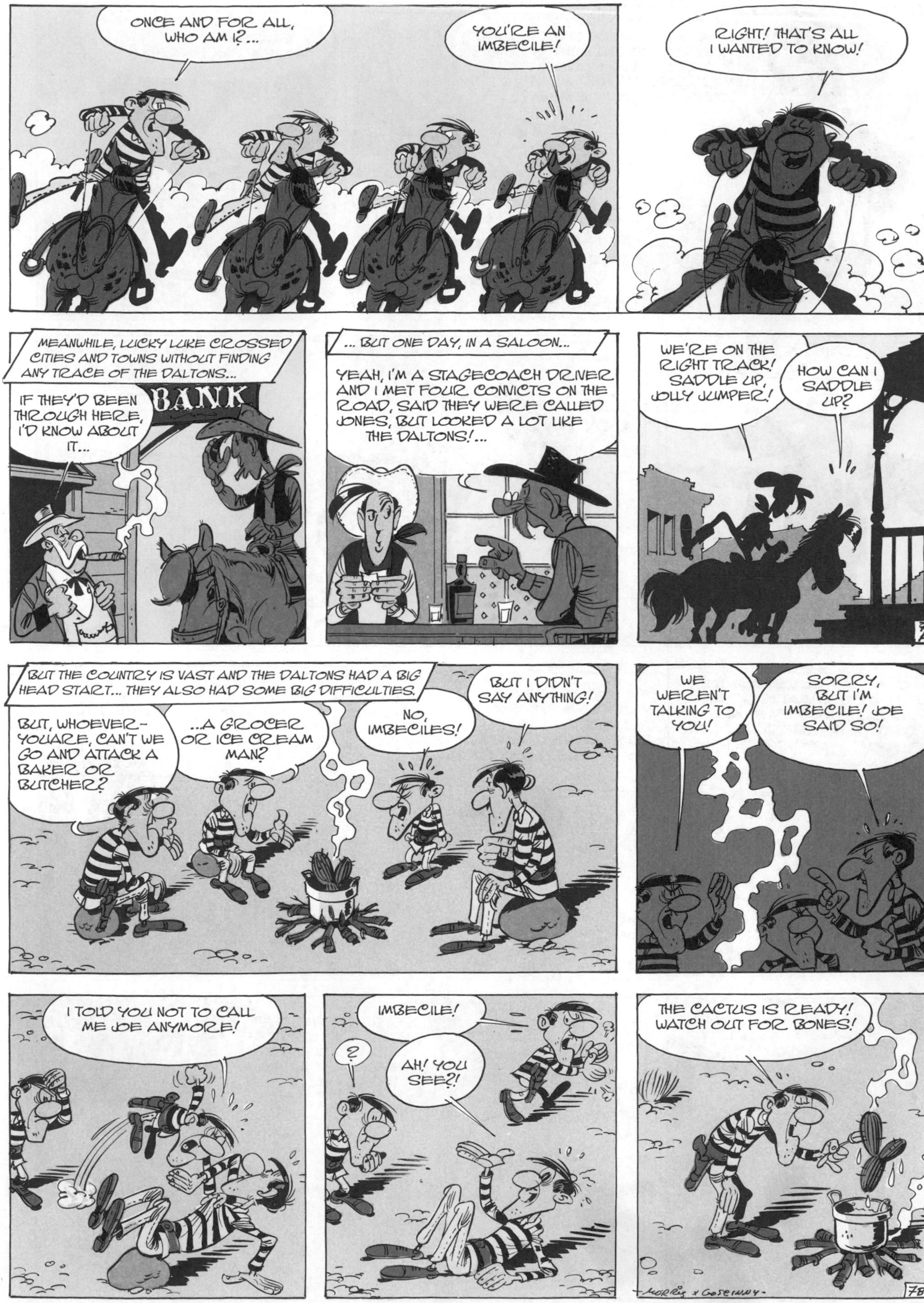
ONCE AND FOR ALL, WHO AM I?...
YOU'RE AN IMBECILE!
RIGHT! THAT'S ALL I WANTED TO KNOW!
MEANWHILE, LUCKY LUKE CROSSED CITIES AND TOWNS WITHOUT FINDING ANY TRACE OF THE DALTONS...
BANK
IF THEY'D BEEN THROUGH HERE, I'D KNOW ABOUT IT...
... BUT ONE DAY, IN A SALOON...
YEAH, I'M A STAGECOACH DRIVER AND I MET FOUR CONVICTS ON THE ROAD, SAID THEY WERE CALLED JONES, BUT LOOKED A LOT LIKE THE DALTONS!...
WE'RE ON THE RIGHT TRACK! SADDLE UP, JOLLY JUMPER!
HOW CAN I SADDLE UP?
BUT THE COUNTRY IS VAST AND THE DALTONS HAD A BIG HEAD START... THEY ALSO HAD SOME BIG DIFFICULTIES.
BUT, WHOEVER-YOUARE, CAN'T WE GO AND ATTACK A BAKER OR BUTCHER?
...A GROCER OR ICE CREAM MAN?
NO, IMBECILES!
BUT I DIDN'T SAY ANYTHING!
WE WEREN'T TALKING TO YOU!
SORRY, BUT I'M IMBECILE! JOE SAID SO!
I TOLD YOU NOT TO CALL ME JOE ANYMORE!
IMBECILE!
?
AH! YOU SEE?!
THE CACTUS IS READY! WATCH OUT FOR BONES!
MORRIS x GOSCINNY
78

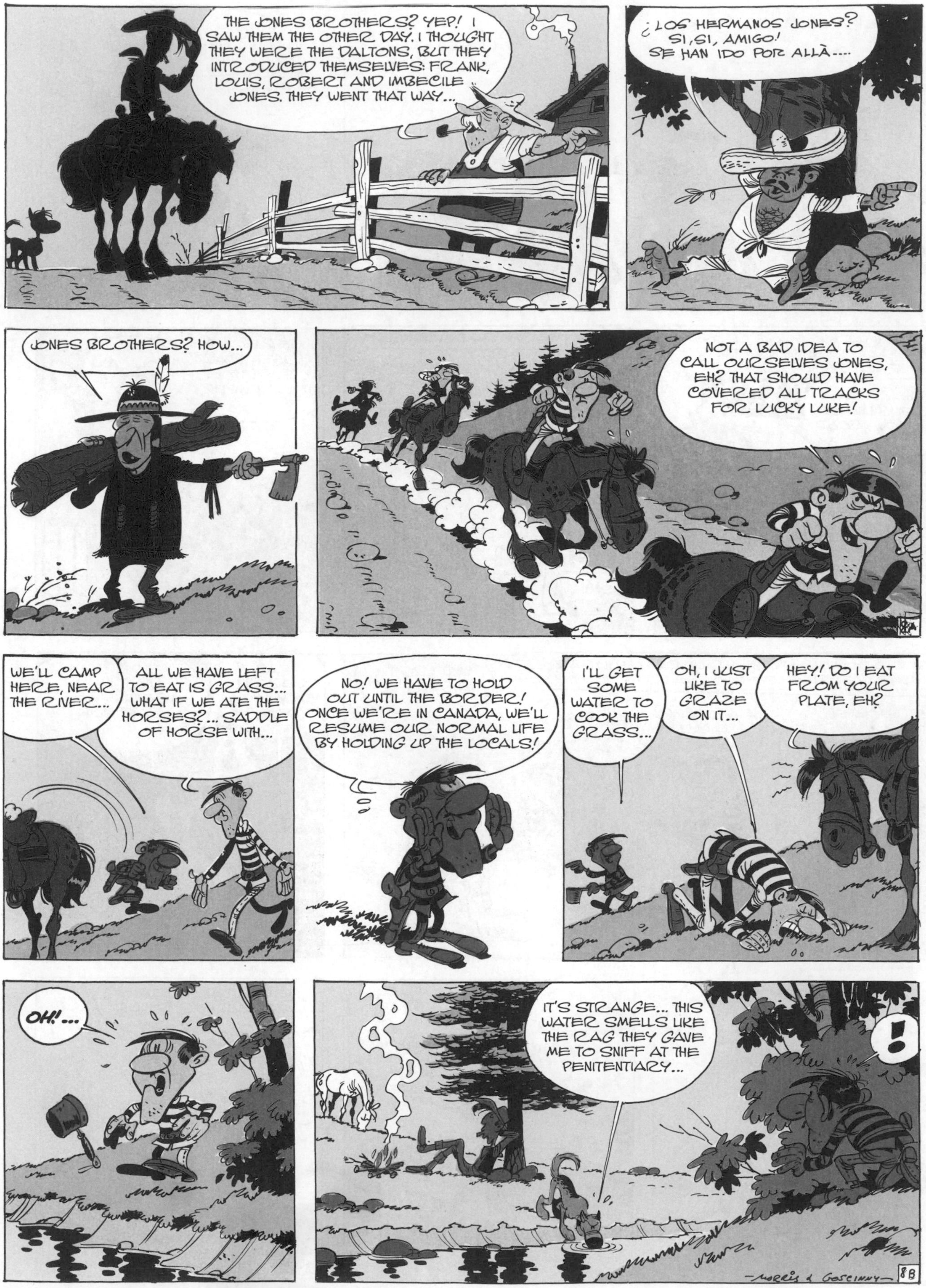
THE JONES BROTHERS? YEP! I SAW THEM THE OTHER DAY. I THOUGHT THEY WERE THE DALTONS, BUT THEY INTRODUCED THEMSELVES: FRANK, LOUIS, ROBERT AND IMBECILE JONES. THEY WENT THAT WAY...
¿LOS HERMANOS JONES? SI, SI, AMIGO! SE HAN IDO POR ALLÀ....
JONES BROTHERS? HOW...
NOT A BAD IDEA TO CALL OURSELVES JONES, EH? THAT SHOULD HAVE COVERED ALL TRACKS FOR LUCKY LUKE!
WE'LL CAMP HERE, NEAR THE RIVER...
ALL WE HAVE LEFT TO EAT IS GRASS... WHAT IF WE ATE THE HORSES?... SADDLE OF HORSE WITH...
NO! WE HAVE TO HOLD OUT UNTIL THE BORDER! ONCE WE'RE IN CANADA, WE'LL RESUME OUR NORMAL LIFE BY HOLDING UP THE LOCALS!
I'LL GET SOME WATER TO COOK THE GRASS...
OH, I JUST LIKE TO GRAZE ON IT...
HEY! DO I EAT FROM YOUR PLATE, EH?
OH!...
IT'S STRANGE... THIS WATER SMELLS LIKE THE RAG THEY GAVE ME TO SNIFF AT THE PENITENTIARY...
!
MORRIS & GOSCINNY
8B

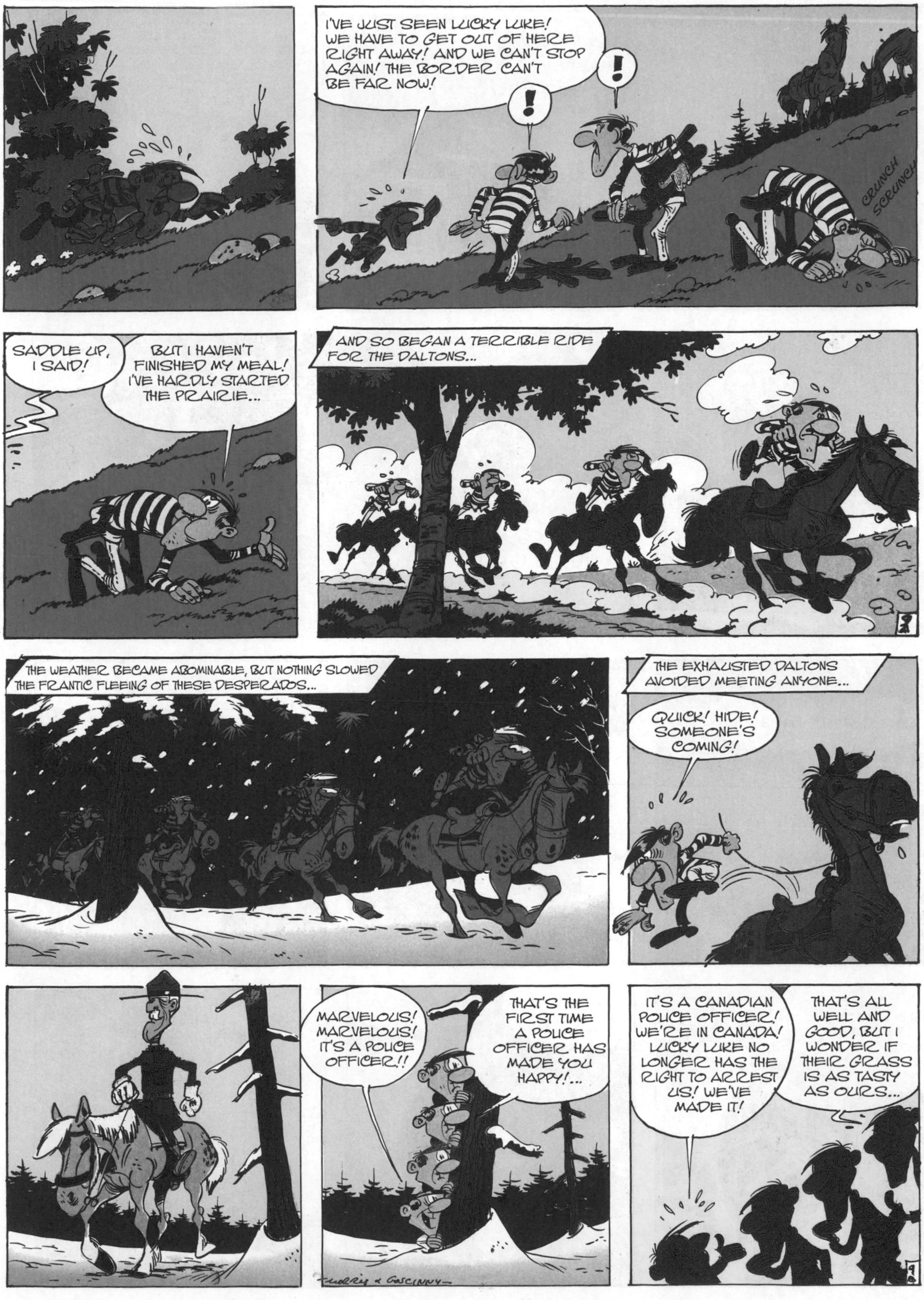
I'VE JUST SEEN LUCKY LUKE! WE HAVE TO GET OUT OF HERE RIGHT AWAY! AND WE CAN'T STOP AGAIN! THE BORDER CAN'T BE FAR NOW!
!
!
CRUNCH
SCRUNCH
SADDLE UP, I SAID!
BUT I HAVEN'T FINISHED MY MEAL! I'VE HARDLY STARTED THE PRAIRIE...
AND SO BEGAN A TERRIBLE RIDE FOR THE DALTONS...
THE WEATHER BECAME ABOMINABLE, BUT NOTHING SLOWED THE FRANTIC FLEEING OF THESE DESPERADOS...
THE EXHAUSTED DALTONS AVOIDED MEETING ANYONE...
QUICK! HIDE! SOMEONE'S COMING!
MARVELOUS! MARVELOUS! IT'S A POLICE OFFICER!!
THAT'S THE FIRST TIME A POLICE OFFICER HAS MADE YOU HAPPY!...
IT'S A CANADIAN POLICE OFFICER! WE'RE IN CANADA! LUCKY LUKE NO LONGER HAS THE RIGHT TO ARREST US! WE'VE MADE IT!
THAT'S ALL WELL AND GOOD, BUT I WONDER IF THEIR GRASS IS AS TASTY AS OURS...

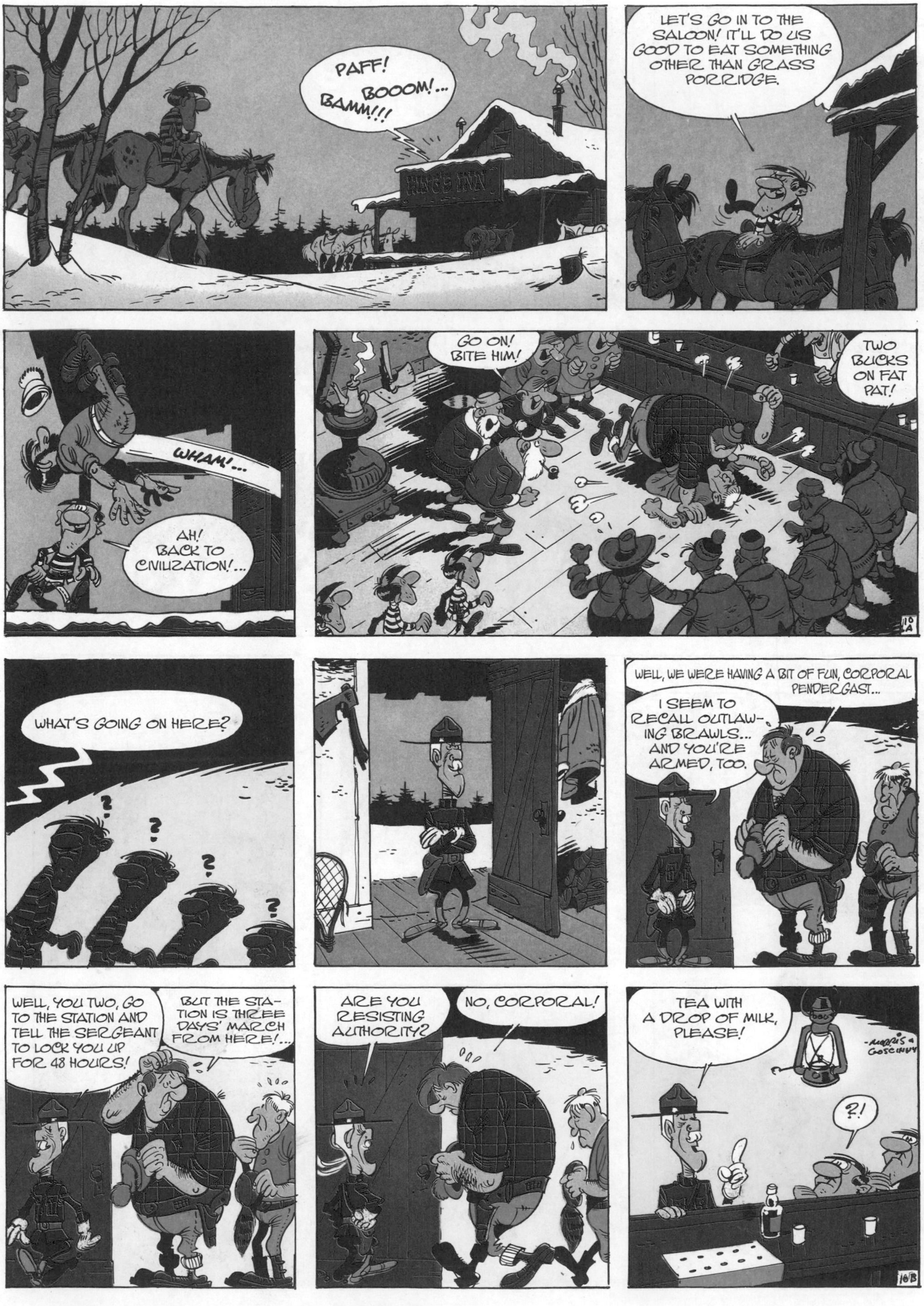
PAFF!
BOOOM!...
BAMM!!!
LET'S GO IN TO THE SALOON! IT'LL DO US GOOD TO EAT SOMETHING OTHER THAN GRASS PORRIDGE.
WHAM!...
AH! BACK TO CIVILIZATION!...
GO ON! BITE HIM!
TWO BUCKS ON FAT PAT!
WHAT'S GOING ON HERE?
WELL, WE WERE HAVING A BIT OF FUN, CORPORAL PENDERGAST...
I SEEM TO RECALL OUTLAWING BRAWLS... AND YOU'RE ARMED, TOO.
WELL, YOU TWO, GO TO THE STATION AND TELL THE SERGEANT TO LOCK YOU UP FOR 48 HOURS!
BUT THE STATION IS THREE DAYS' MARCH FROM HERE!...
ARE YOU RESISTING AUTHORITY?
NO, CORPORAL!
TEA WITH A DROP OF MILK, PLEASE!
?!
MORRIS & GOSCINNY

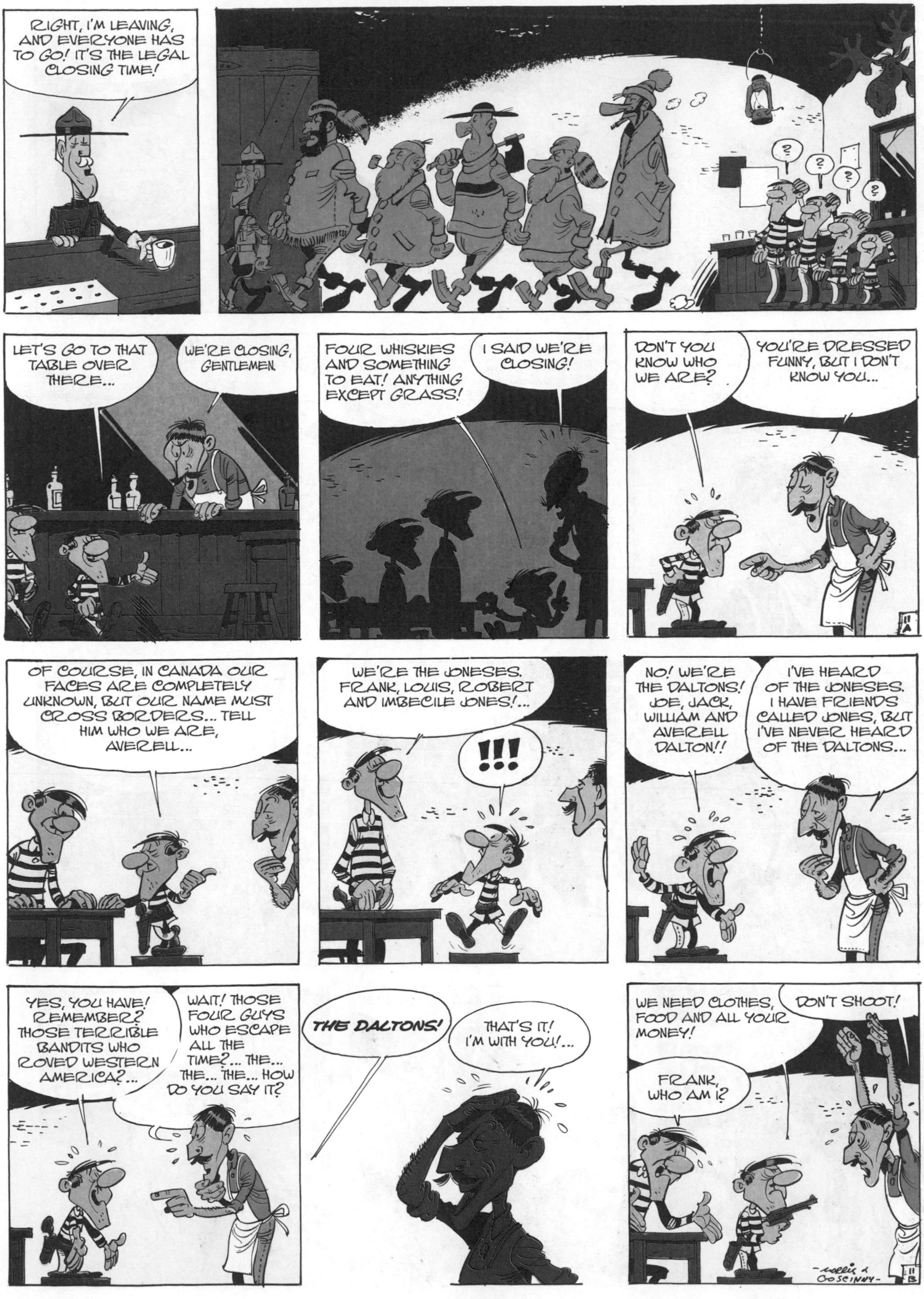
RIGHT, I'M LEAVING, AND EVERYONE HAS TO GO! IT'S THE LEGAL CLOSING TIME!
LET'S GO TO THAT TABLE OVER THERE...
WE'RE CLOSING, GENTLEMEN.
FOUR WHISKIES AND SOMETHING TO EAT! ANYTHING EXCEPT GRASS!
I SAID WE'RE CLOSING!
DON'T YOU KNOW WHO WE ARE?
YOU'RE DRESSED FUNNY, BUT I DON'T KNOW YOU...
OF COURSE, IN CANADA OUR FACES ARE COMPLETELY UNKNOWN, BUT OUR NAME MUST CROSS BORDERS... TELL HIM WHO WE ARE, AVERELL...
WE'RE THE JONESES. FRANK, LOUIS, ROBERT AND IMBECILE JONES!...
!!!
NO! WE'RE THE DALTONS! JOE, JACK, WILLIAM AND AVERELL DALTON!!
I'VE HEARD OF THE JONESES. I HAVE FRIENDS CALLED JONES, BUT I'VE NEVER HEARD OF THE DALTONS...
YES, YOU HAVE! REMEMBER? THOSE TERRIBLE BANDITS WHO ROVED WESTERN AMERICA?...
WAIT! THOSE FOUR GUYS WHO ESCAPE ALL THE TIME?... THE... THE... THE... HOW DO YOU SAY IT?
THE DALTONS!
THAT'S IT! I'M WITH YOU!...
WE NEED CLOTHES, FOOD AND ALL YOUR MONEY!
DON'T SHOOT!
FRANK, WHO AM I?
-MORRIS & GOSCINNY-

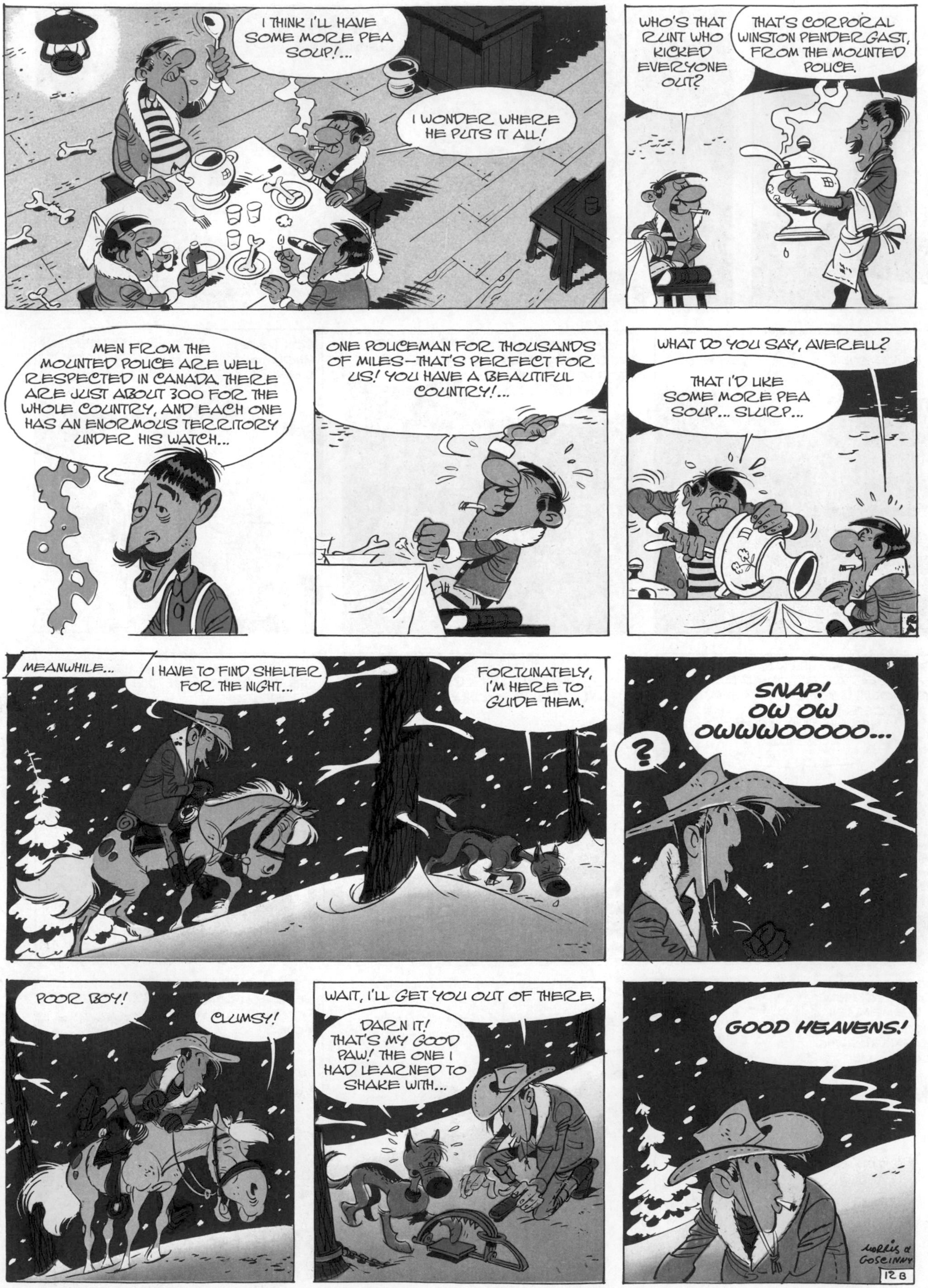

I THINK I'LL HAVE SOME MORE PEA SOUP!...
I WONDER WHERE HE PUTS IT ALL!
WHO'S THAT RUNT WHO KICKED EVERYONE OUT?
THAT'S CORPORAL WINSTON PENDERGAST, FROM THE MOUNTED POLICE.
MEN FROM THE MOUNTED POLICE ARE WELL RESPECTED IN CANADA. THERE ARE JUST ABOUT 300 FOR THE WHOLE COUNTRY, AND EACH ONE HAS AN ENORMOUS TERRITORY UNDER HIS WATCH...
ONE POLICEMAN FOR THOUSANDS OF MILES—THAT'S PERFECT FOR US! YOU HAVE A BEAUTIFUL COUNTRY!...
WHAT DO YOU SAY, AVERELL?
THAT I'D LIKE SOME MORE PEA SOUP... SLURP...
MEANWHILE...
I HAVE TO FIND SHELTER FOR THE NIGHT...
FORTUNATELY, I'M HERE TO GUIDE THEM.
SNAP! OW OW OWWWOOOOO...
?
POOR BOY!
CLUMSY!
WAIT, I'LL GET YOU OUT OF THERE.
DARN IT! THAT'S MY GOOD PAW! THE ONE I HAD LEARNED TO SHAKE WITH...
GOOD HEAVENS!
MORRIS & GOSCINNY
12 B

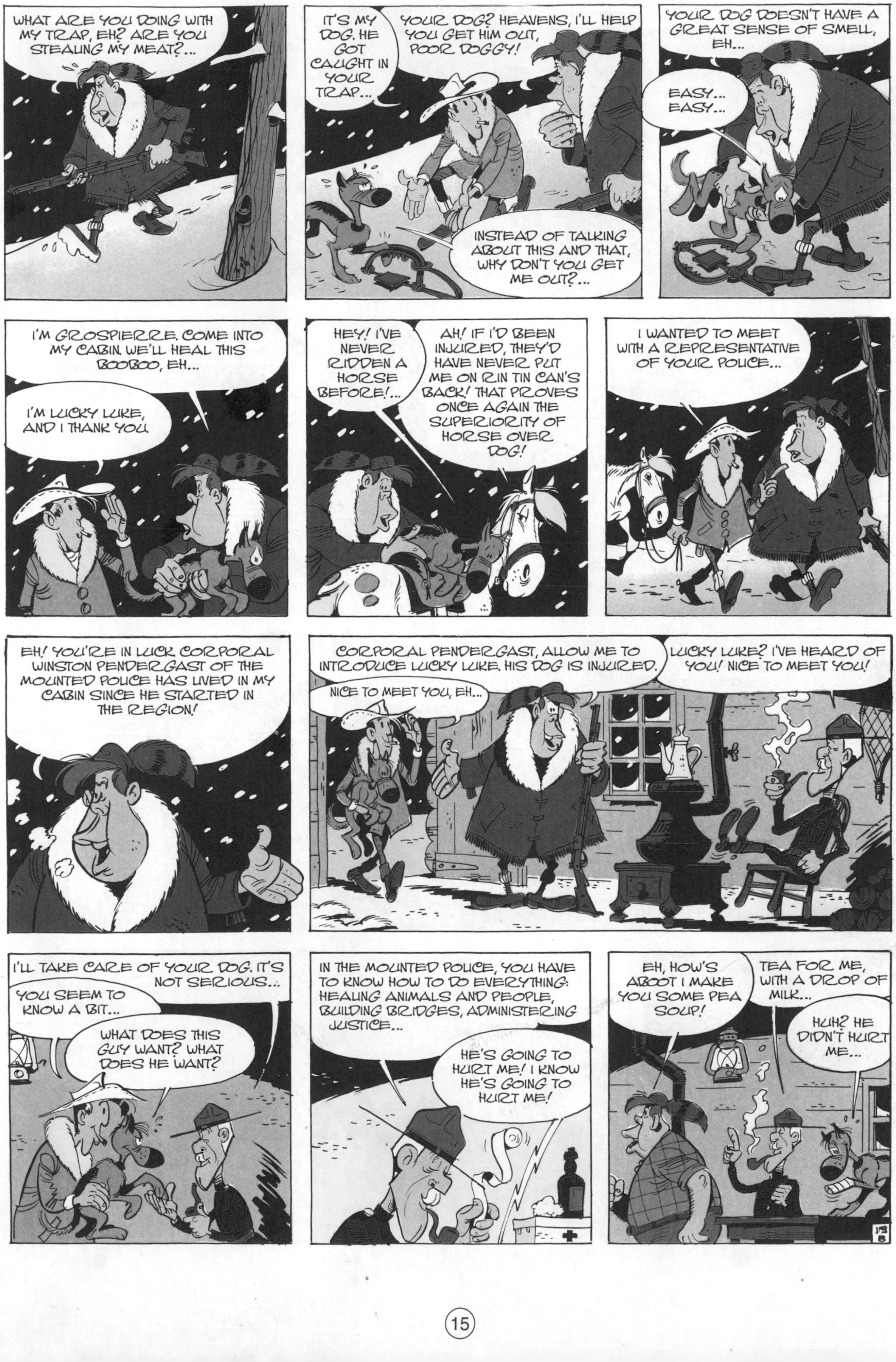
WHAT ARE YOU DOING WITH MY TRAP, EH? ARE YOU STEALING MY MEAT?...
IT'S MY DOG. HE GOT CAUGHT IN YOUR TRAP...
YOUR DOG? HEAVENS, I'LL HELP YOU GET HIM OUT, POOR DOGGY!
INSTEAD OF TALKING ABOUT THIS AND THAT, WHY DON'T YOU GET ME OUT?...
YOUR DOG DOESN'T HAVE A GREAT SENSE OF SMELL, EH...
EASY... EASY...
I'M GROSPIERRE. COME INTO MY CABIN. WE'LL HEAL THIS BOOBOO, EH...
I'M LUCKY LUKE, AND I THANK YOU.
HEY! I'VE NEVER RIDDEN A HORSE BEFORE!...
AH! IF I'D BEEN INJURED, THEY'D HAVE NEVER PUT ME ON RIN TIN CAN'S BACK! THAT PROVES ONCE AGAIN THE SUPERIORITY OF HORSE OVER DOG!
I WANTED TO MEET WITH A REPRESENTATIVE OF YOUR POLICE...
EH! YOU'RE IN LUCK. CORPORAL WINSTON PENDERGAST OF THE MOUNTED POLICE HAS LIVED IN MY CABIN SINCE HE STARTED IN THE REGION!
CORPORAL PENDERGAST, ALLOW ME TO INTRODUCE LUCKY LUKE. HIS DOG IS INJURED.
NICE TO MEET YOU, EH...
LUCKY LUKE? I'VE HEARD OF YOU! NICE TO MEET YOU!
I'LL TAKE CARE OF YOUR DOG. IT'S NOT SERIOUS...
YOU SEEM TO KNOW A BIT...
WHAT DOES THIS GUY WANT? WHAT DOES HE WANT?
IN THE MOUNTED POLICE, YOU HAVE TO KNOW HOW TO DO EVERYTHING: HEALING ANIMALS AND PEOPLE, BUILDING BRIDGES, ADMINISTERING JUSTICE...
HE'S GOING TO HURT ME! I KNOW HE'S GOING TO HURT ME!
EH, HOW'S ABOOT I MAKE YOU SOME PEA SOUP!
TEA FOR ME, WITH A DROP OF MILK...
HUH? HE DIDN'T HURT ME...

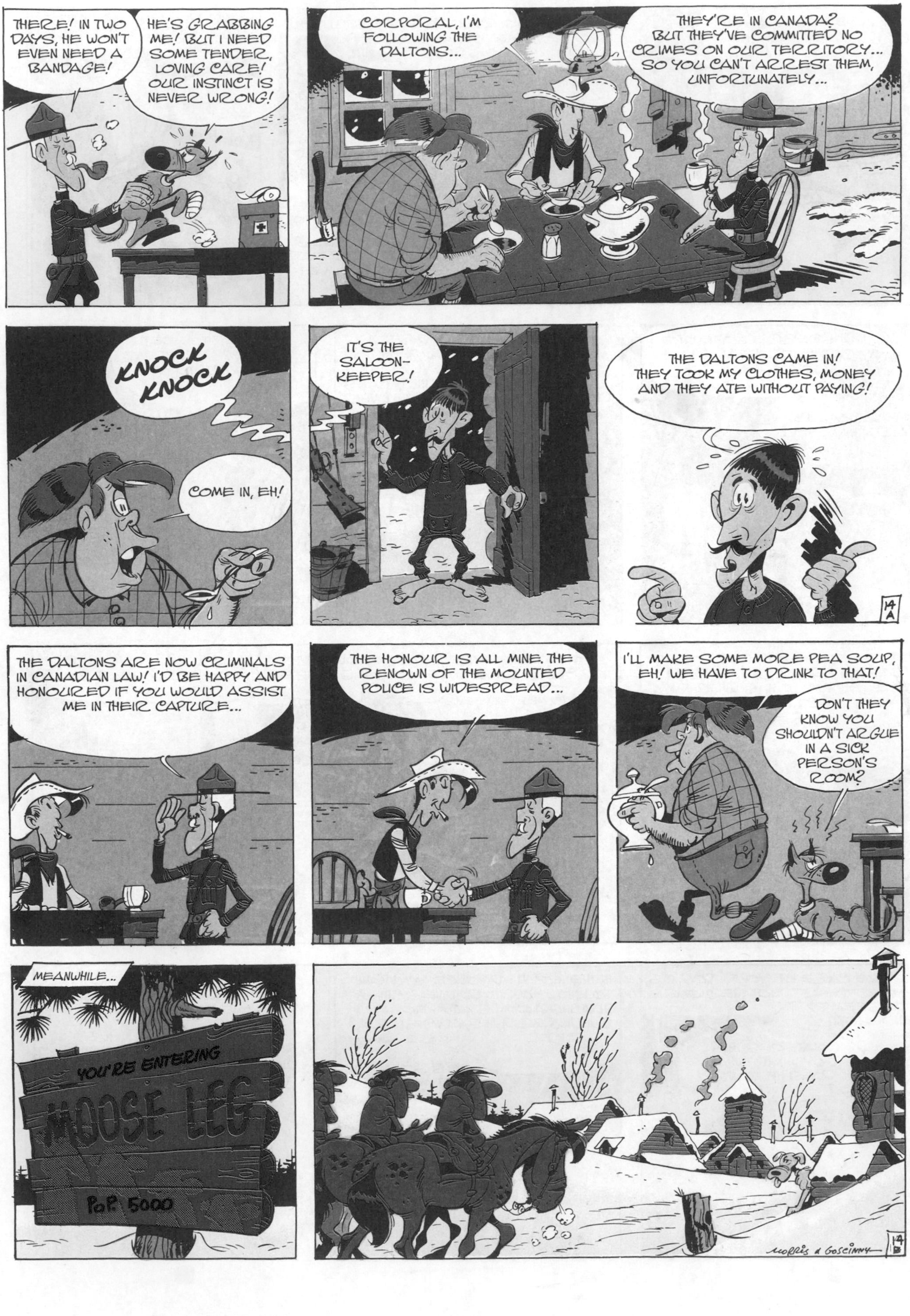
THERE! IN TWO DAYS, HE WON'T EVEN NEED A BANDAGE!
HE'S GRABBING ME! BUT I NEED SOME TENDER, LOVING CARE! OUR INSTINCT IS NEVER WRONG!
CORPORAL, I'M FOLLOWING THE DALTONS...
THEY'RE IN CANADA? BUT THEY'VE COMMITTED NO CRIMES ON OUR TERRITORY... SO YOU CAN'T ARREST THEM, UNFORTUNATELY...
KNOCK KNOCK
COME IN, EH!
IT'S THE SALOON-KEEPER!
THE DALTONS CAME IN! THEY TOOK MY CLOTHES, MONEY AND THEY ATE WITHOUT PAYING!
14 A
THE DALTONS ARE NOW CRIMINALS IN CANADIAN LAW! I'D BE HAPPY AND HONOURED IF YOU WOULD ASSIST ME IN THEIR CAPTURE...
THE HONOUR IS ALL MINE. THE RENOWN OF THE MOUNTED POLICE IS WIDESPREAD...
I'LL MAKE SOME MORE PEA SOUP, EH! WE HAVE TO DRINK TO THAT!
DON'T THEY KNOW YOU SHOULDN'T ARGUE IN A SICK PERSON'S ROOM?
MEANWHILE...
YOU'RE ENTERING
MOOSE LEG
POP. 5000
MORRIS & GOSCINNY
14 B

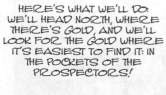

HERE'S WHAT WE'LL DO: WE'LL HEAD NORTH, WHERE THERE'S GOLD, AND WE'LL LOOK FOR THE GOLD WHERE IT'S EASIEST TO FIND IT: IN THE POCKETS OF THE PROSPECTORS!

NOW LET'S START TO MAKE SOME PROFIT, AND MAKE OUR NAME FAMOUS TOO!

JONES?

NO! DALTON! LET'S GO! LET'S ATTACK THE BANK!

EXCELLENT! IT'S ONLY THROUGH WORK THAT ONE CAN BE TRULY SATISFIED!

YOU ARE LEAVING MOOSE LEG

AND THE DALTONS' RENOWN GREW NON-STOP...

IT WAS THE DALTONS THAT DID IT!

THE WHO?

MOOSE LEG BANK

IN HAMANEGG...

IT WAS THE DALTONS THAT ATTACKED ME!

I'VE ALREADY HEARD THAT NAME SOMEWHERE...

HAMANEGG BANK!

IN BRISTOLBRIDGE...

IT WOULDN'T BE THE DALTONS THAT DID THIS TO YOU?

BRISTOLBRIDGE BANK

FINALLY, IN LITTLEBRICK...

YOU'RE THE DALTONS! TAKE IT ALL! DON'T SHOOT!!

IN LITTLEBRICK, WHERE A FEW OF OUR FRIENDS TURNED UP...

THE DALTONS HAVE MADE THEMSELVES FAMOUS IN NO TIME AT ALL!...

AND THE BAD THING IS THAT YOUR COUNTRY IS ENORMOUS! IT WON'T BE EASY TO GET A HOLD ON THEM!

INDEED, MY DEAR COLLEAGUE, MY FATHER WAS A PUREBRED ENGLISH STALLION.

MINE HAD INDIAN BLOOD.

LET'S TAKE A DRINK...

I'M NOT ALLOWED TO SMOKE OR DRINK ON DUTY, BUT PERHAPS A LITTLE TEA WITH A DROP OF MILK...

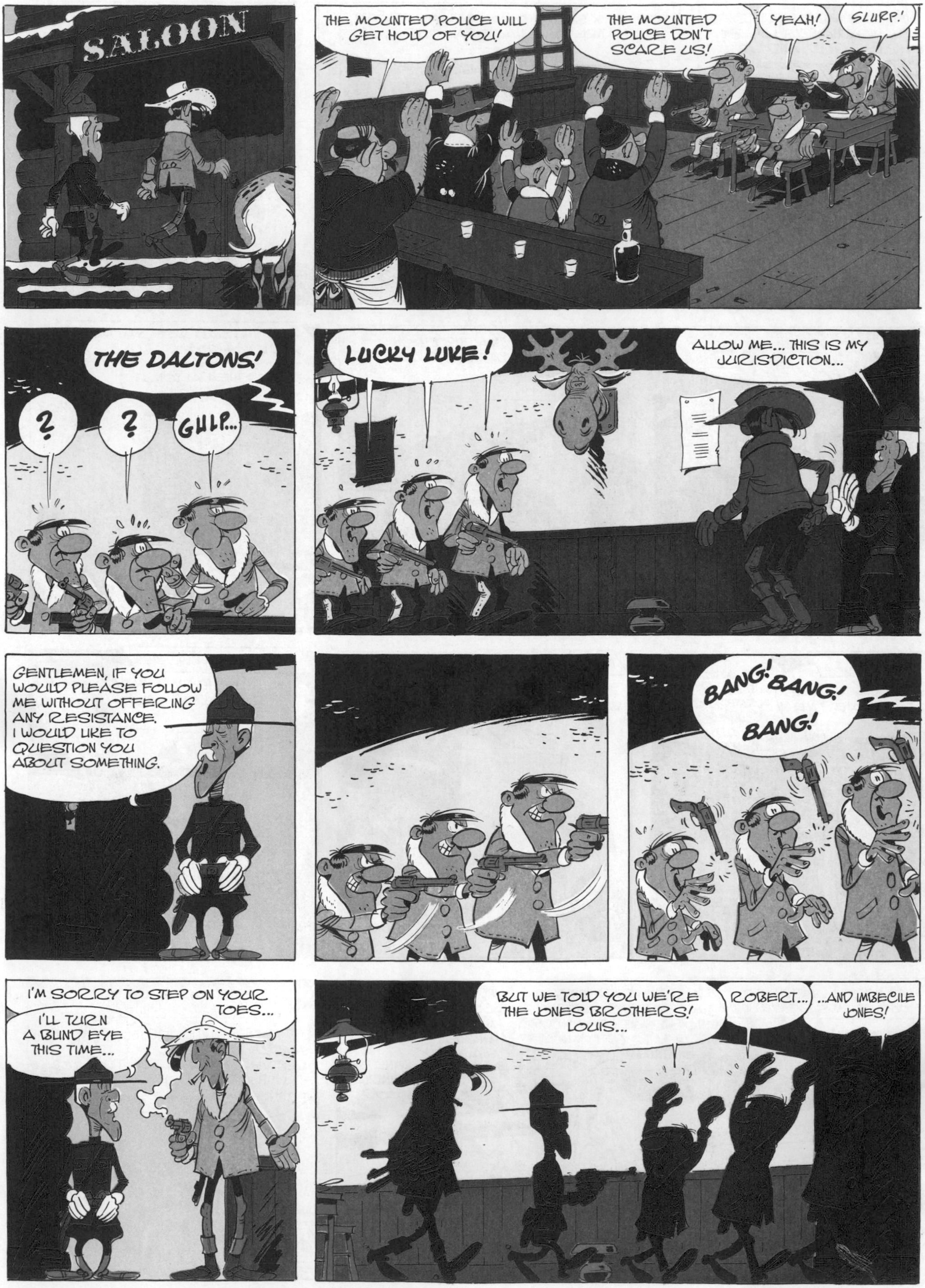
SALOON
THE MOUNTED POLICE WILL GET HOLD OF YOU!
THE MOUNTED POLICE DON'T SCARE US!
YEAH!
SLURP!
THE DALTONS!
?
?
GULP...
LUCKY LUKE!
ALLOW ME... THIS IS MY JURISDICTION...
GENTLEMEN, IF YOU WOULD PLEASE FOLLOW ME WITHOUT OFFERING ANY RESISTANCE. I WOULD LIKE TO QUESTION YOU ABOUT SOMETHING.
BANG! BANG! BANG!
I'M SORRY TO STEP ON YOUR TOES...
I'LL TURN A BLIND EYE THIS TIME...
BUT WE TOLD YOU WE'RE THE JONES BROTHERS! LOUIS...
ROBERT...
...AND IMBECILE JONES!

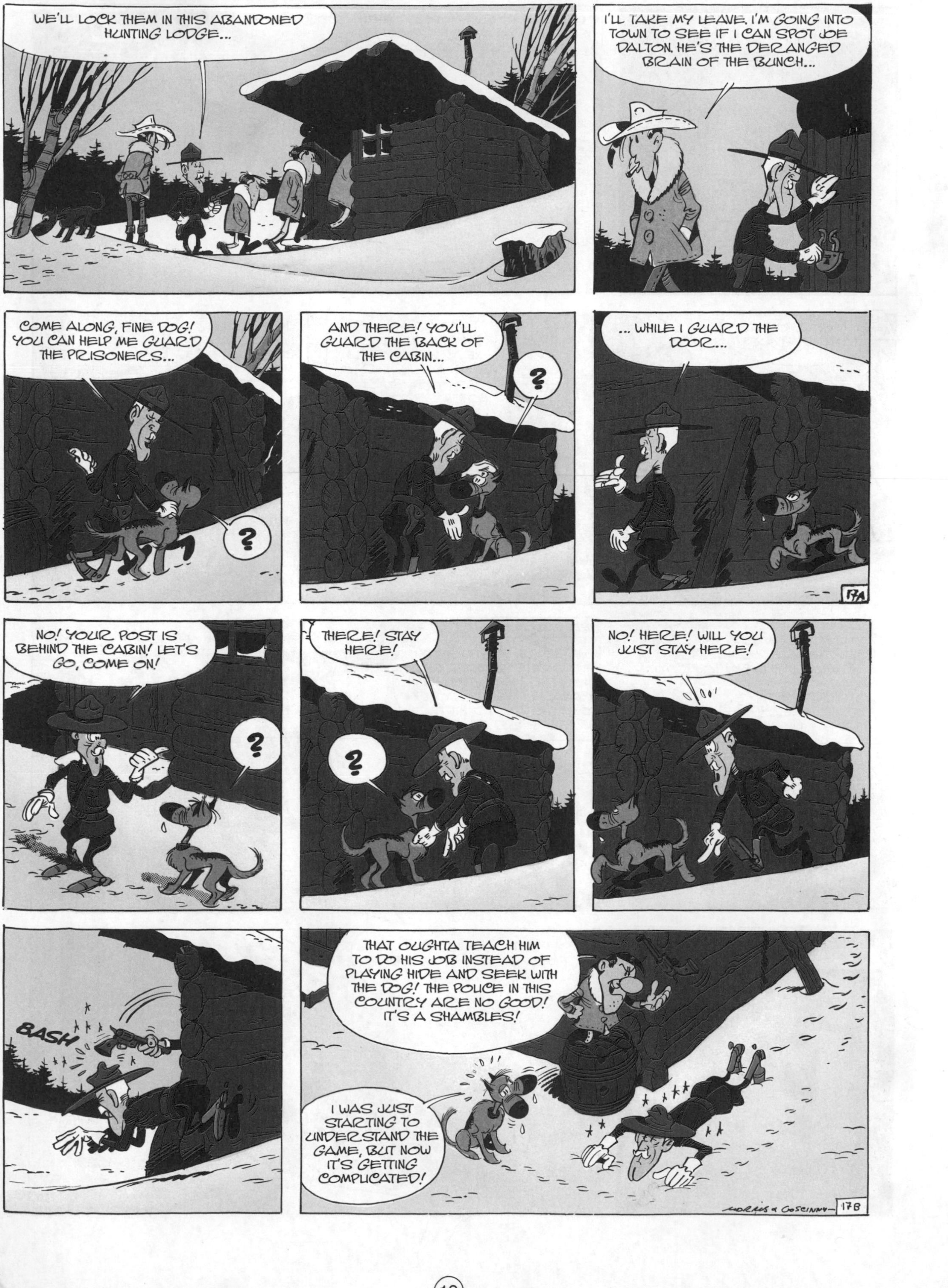

WE'LL LOCK THEM IN THIS ABANDONED HUNTING LODGE...
I'LL TAKE MY LEAVE. I'M GOING INTO TOWN TO SEE IF I CAN SPOT JOE DALTON. HE'S THE DERANGED BRAIN OF THE BUNCH...
COME ALONG, FINE DOG! YOU CAN HELP ME GUARD THE PRISONERS...
?
AND THERE! YOU'LL GUARD THE BACK OF THE CABIN...
?
... WHILE I GUARD THE DOOR...
17A
NO! YOUR POST IS BEHIND THE CABIN! LET'S GO, COME ON!
?
THERE! STAY HERE!
?
NO! HERE! WILL YOU JUST STAY HERE!
BASH
THAT OUGHTA TEACH HIM TO DO HIS JOB INSTEAD OF PLAYING HIDE AND SEEK WITH THE DOG! THE POLICE IN THIS COUNTRY ARE NO GOOD! IT'S A SHAMBLES!
I WAS JUST STARTING TO UNDERSTAND THE GAME, BUT NOW IT'S GETTING COMPLICATED!
MORRIS & GOSCINNY
17B

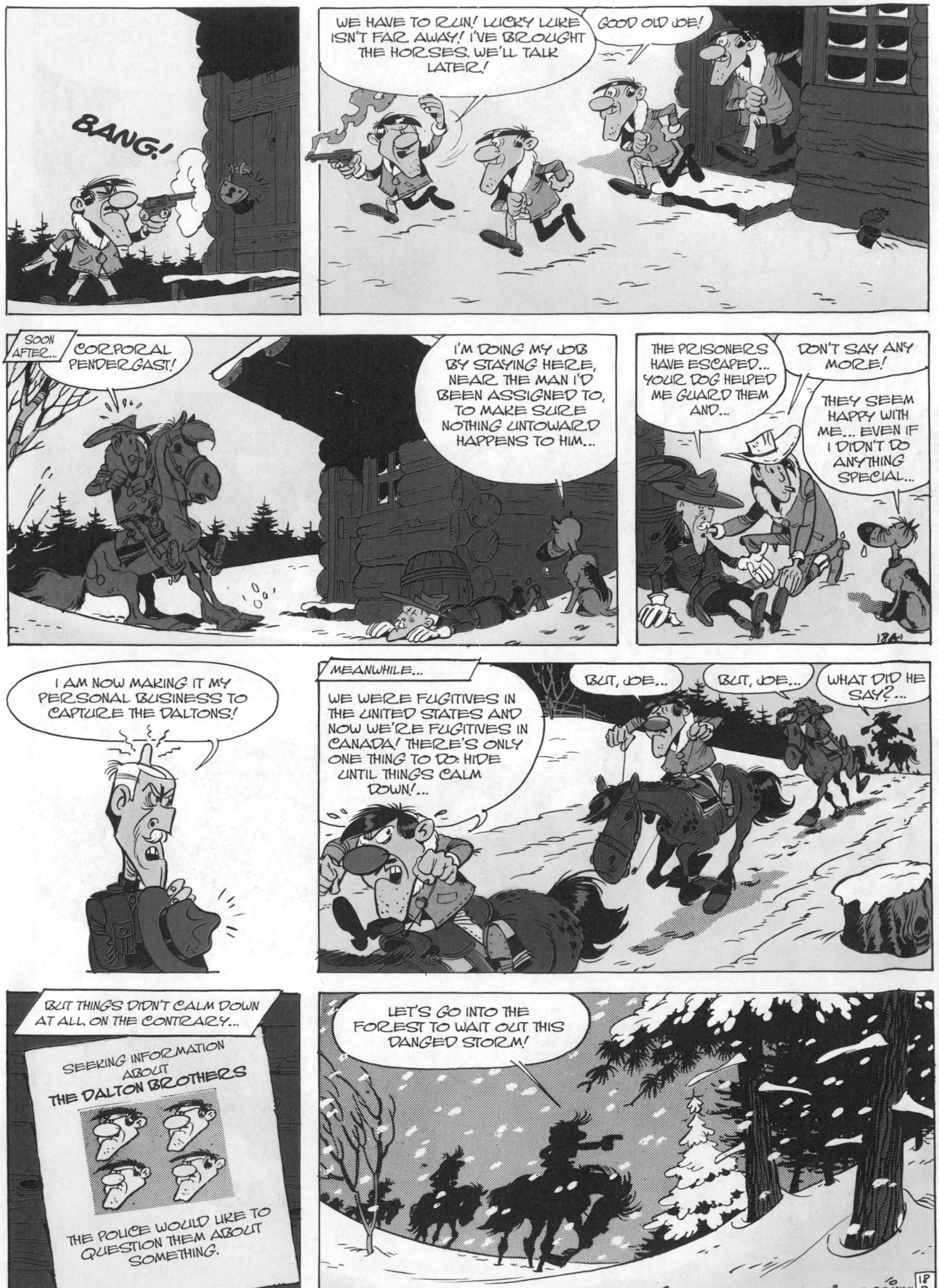
BANG!
WE HAVE TO RUN! LUCKY LUKE ISN'T FAR AWAY! I'VE BROUGHT THE HORSES. WE'LL TALK LATER!
GOOD OLD JOE!
SOON AFTER...
CORPORAL PENDERGAST!
I'M DOING MY JOB BY STAYING HERE, NEAR THE MAN I'D BEEN ASSIGNED TO, TO MAKE SURE NOTHING UNTOWARD HAPPENS TO HIM...
THE PRISONERS HAVE ESCAPED... YOUR DOG HELPED ME GUARD THEM AND...
DON'T SAY ANY MORE!
THEY SEEM HAPPY WITH ME... EVEN IF I DIDN'T DO ANYTHING SPECIAL...
I AM NOW MAKING IT MY PERSONAL BUSINESS TO CAPTURE THE DALTONS!
MEANWHILE...
WE WERE FUGITIVES IN THE UNITED STATES AND NOW WE'RE FUGITIVES IN CANADA! THERE'S ONLY ONE THING TO DO: HIDE UNTIL THINGS CALM DOWN!...
BUT, JOE...
BUT, JOE...
WHAT DID HE SAY?...
BUT THINGS DIDN'T CALM DOWN AT ALL. ON THE CONTRARY...
SEEKING INFORMATION ABOUT
THE DALTON BROTHERS
THE POLICE WOULD LIKE TO QUESTION THEM ABOUT SOMETHING.
LET'S GO INTO THE FOREST TO WAIT OUT THIS DANGED STORM!
MORRIS & GOSCINNY

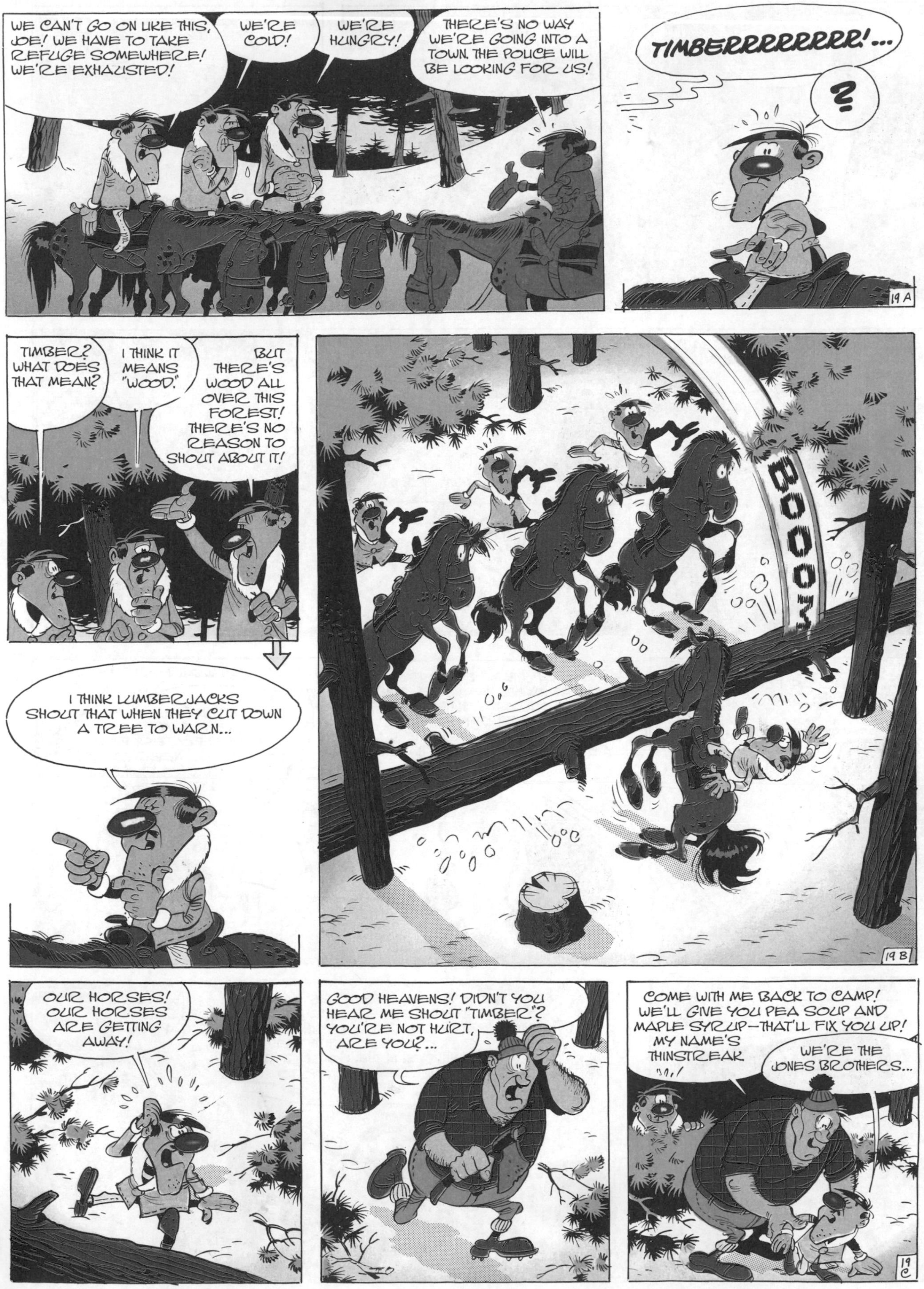

WE CAN'T GO ON LIKE THIS, JOE! WE HAVE TO TAKE REFUGE SOMEWHERE! WE'RE EXHAUSTED!
WE'RE COLD!
WE'RE HUNGRY!
THERE'S NO WAY WE'RE GOING INTO A TOWN. THE POLICE WILL BE LOOKING FOR US!
TIMBERRRRRRRR!...
?
19 A
TIMBER? WHAT DOES THAT MEAN?
I THINK IT MEANS "WOOD."
BUT THERE'S WOOD ALL OVER THIS FOREST! THERE'S NO REASON TO SHOUT ABOUT IT!
I THINK LUMBERJACKS SHOUT THAT WHEN THEY CUT DOWN A TREE TO WARN...
BOOOOM
19 B
OUR HORSES! OUR HORSES ARE GETTING AWAY!
GOOD HEAVENS! DIDN'T YOU HEAR ME SHOUT "TIMBER"? YOU'RE NOT HURT, ARE YOU?...
COME WITH ME BACK TO CAMP! WE'LL GIVE YOU PEA SOUP AND MAPLE SYRUP—THAT'LL FIX YOU UP! MY NAME'S THINSTREAK
WE'RE THE JONES BROTHERS...
19 C

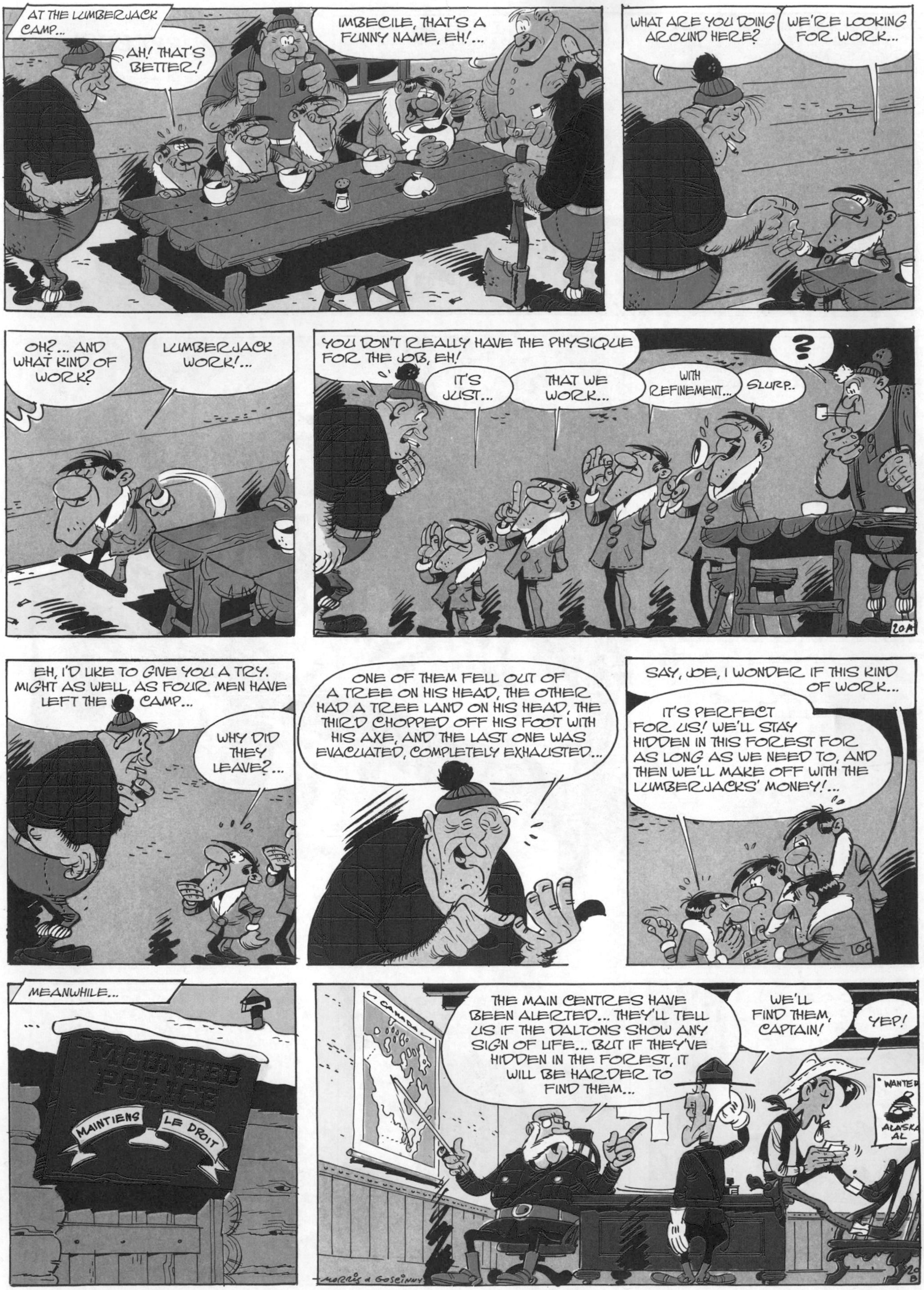
AT THE LUMBERJACK CAMP...
AH! THAT'S BETTER!
IMBECILE, THAT'S A FUNNY NAME, EH!...
WHAT ARE YOU DOING AROUND HERE?
WE'RE LOOKING FOR WORK...
OH?... AND WHAT KIND OF WORK?
LUMBERJACK WORK!...
YOU DON'T REALLY HAVE THE PHYSIQUE FOR THE JOB, EH!
?
IT'S JUST...
THAT WE WORK...
WITH REFINEMENT...
SLURP..
EH, I'D LIKE TO GIVE YOU A TRY. MIGHT AS WELL, AS FOUR MEN HAVE LEFT THE CAMP...
WHY DID THEY LEAVE?...
ONE OF THEM FELL OUT OF A TREE ON HIS HEAD, THE OTHER HAD A TREE LAND ON HIS HEAD, THE THIRD CHOPPED OFF HIS FOOT WITH HIS AXE, AND THE LAST ONE WAS EVACUATED, COMPLETELY EXHAUSTED...
SAY, JOE, I WONDER IF THIS KIND OF WORK...
IT'S PERFECT FOR US! WE'LL STAY HIDDEN IN THIS FOREST FOR AS LONG AS WE NEED TO, AND THEN WE'LL MAKE OFF WITH THE LUMBERJACKS' MONEY!...
MEANWHILE...
MOUNTED POLICE
MAINTIENS LE DROIT
CANADA
THE MAIN CENTRES HAVE BEEN ALERTED... THEY'LL TELL US IF THE DALTONS SHOW ANY SIGN OF LIFE... BUT IF THEY'VE HIDDEN IN THE FOREST, IT WILL BE HARDER TO FIND THEM...
WE'LL FIND THEM, CAPTAIN!
YEP!
WANTED
ALASKA AL

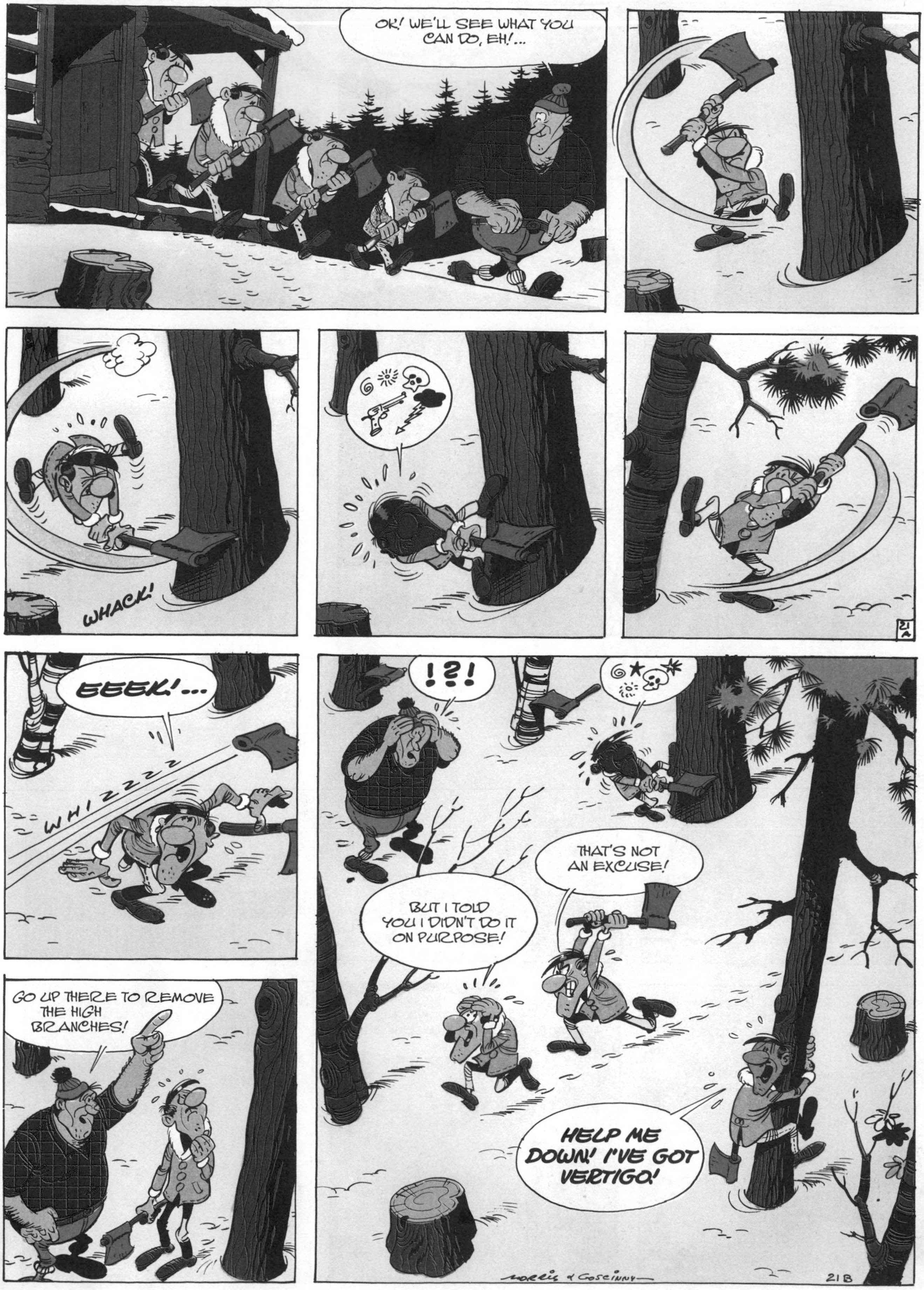
OK! WE'LL SEE WHAT YOU CAN DO, EH!...
WHACK!
21A
EEEK!...
WHIZZZZZ
!?!
BUT I TOLD YOU I DIDN'T DO IT ON PURPOSE!
THAT'S NOT AN EXCUSE!
GO UP THERE TO REMOVE THE HIGH BRANCHES!
HELP ME DOWN! I'VE GOT VERTIGO!
MORRIS & GOSCINNY
21B

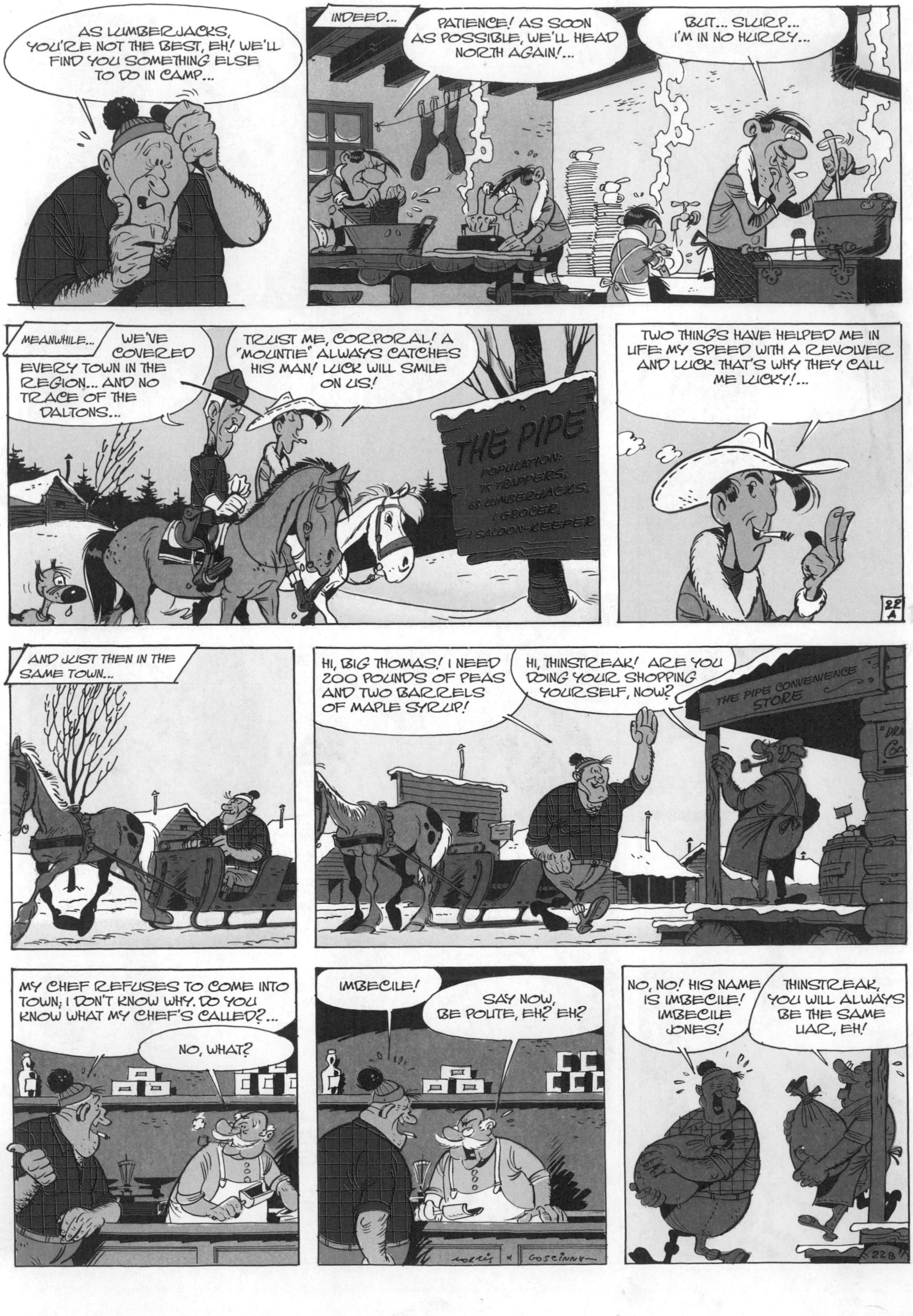
AS LUMBERJACKS, YOU'RE NOT THE BEST, EH! WE'LL FIND YOU SOMETHING ELSE TO DO IN CAMP...
INDEED...
PATIENCE! AS SOON AS POSSIBLE, WE'LL HEAD NORTH AGAIN!...
BUT... SLURP... I'M IN NO HURRY...
MEANWHILE...
WE'VE COVERED EVERY TOWN IN THE REGION... AND NO TRACE OF THE DALTONS...
TRUST ME, CORPORAL! A "MOUNTIE" ALWAYS CATCHES HIS MAN! LUCK WILL SMILE ON US!
THE PIPE
POPULATION:
TRAPPERS,
LUMBERJACKS,
1 GROCER,
1 SALOON-KEEPER
TWO THINGS HAVE HELPED ME IN LIFE: MY SPEED WITH A REVOLVER AND LUCK THAT'S WHY THEY CALL ME LUCKY!...
AND JUST THEN IN THE SAME TOWN...
HI, BIG THOMAS! I NEED 200 POUNDS OF PEAS AND TWO BARRELS OF MAPLE SYRUP!
HI, THINSTREAK! ARE YOU DOING YOUR SHOPPING YOURSELF, NOW?
THE PIPE CONVENIENCE STORE
MY CHEF REFUSES TO COME INTO TOWN; I DON'T KNOW WHY. DO YOU KNOW WHAT MY CHEF'S CALLED?...
NO, WHAT?
IMBECILE!
SAY NOW, BE POLITE, EH? EH?
NO, NO! HIS NAME IS IMBECILE! IMBECILE JONES!
THINSTREAK, YOU WILL ALWAYS BE THE SAME LIAR, EH!

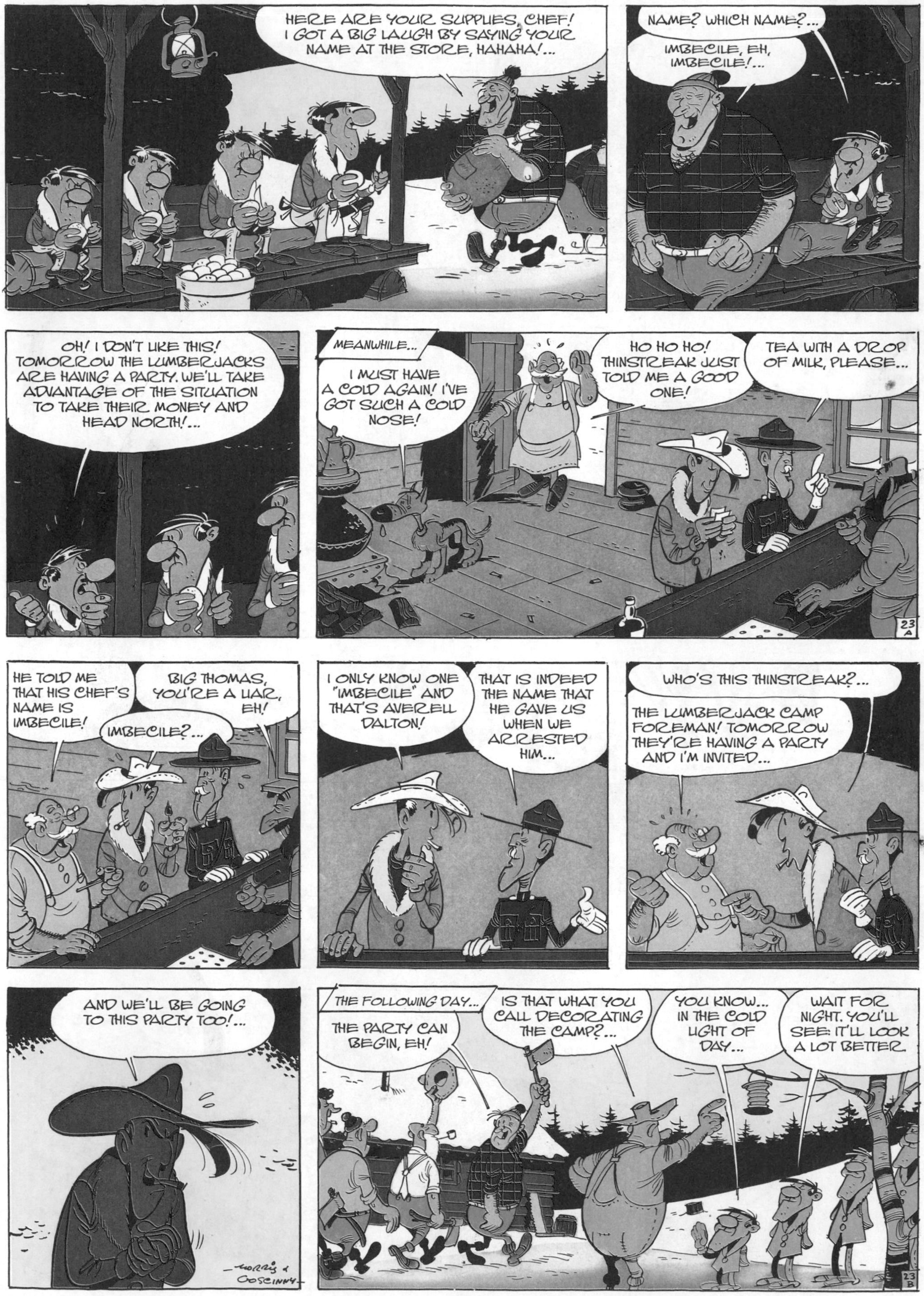
HERE ARE YOUR SUPPLIES, CHEF! I GOT A BIG LAUGH BY SAYING YOUR NAME AT THE STORE, HAHAHA!...
NAME? WHICH NAME?...
IMBECILE, EH, IMBECILE!...
OH! I DON'T LIKE THIS! TOMORROW THE LUMBERJACKS ARE HAVING A PARTY. WE'LL TAKE ADVANTAGE OF THE SITUATION TO TAKE THEIR MONEY AND HEAD NORTH!...
MEANWHILE...
I MUST HAVE A COLD AGAIN! I'VE GOT SUCH A COLD NOSE!
HO HO HO! THINSTREAK JUST TOLD ME A GOOD ONE!
TEA WITH A DROP OF MILK, PLEASE...
23 A
HE TOLD ME THAT HIS CHEF'S NAME IS IMBECILE!
BIG THOMAS, YOU'RE A LIAR, EH!
IMBECILE?...
I ONLY KNOW ONE "IMBECILE" AND THAT'S AVERELL DALTON!
THAT IS INDEED THE NAME THAT HE GAVE US WHEN WE ARRESTED HIM...
WHO'S THIS THINSTREAK?...
THE LUMBERJACK CAMP FOREMAN! TOMORROW THEY'RE HAVING A PARTY AND I'M INVITED...
AND WE'LL BE GOING TO THIS PARTY TOO!...
MORRIS & GOSCINNY
THE FOLLOWING DAY...
THE PARTY CAN BEGIN, EH!
IS THAT WHAT YOU CALL DECORATING THE CAMP?...
YOU KNOW... IN THE COLD LIGHT OF DAY...
WAIT FOR NIGHT. YOU'LL SEE: IT'LL LOOK A LOT BETTER.
23 B

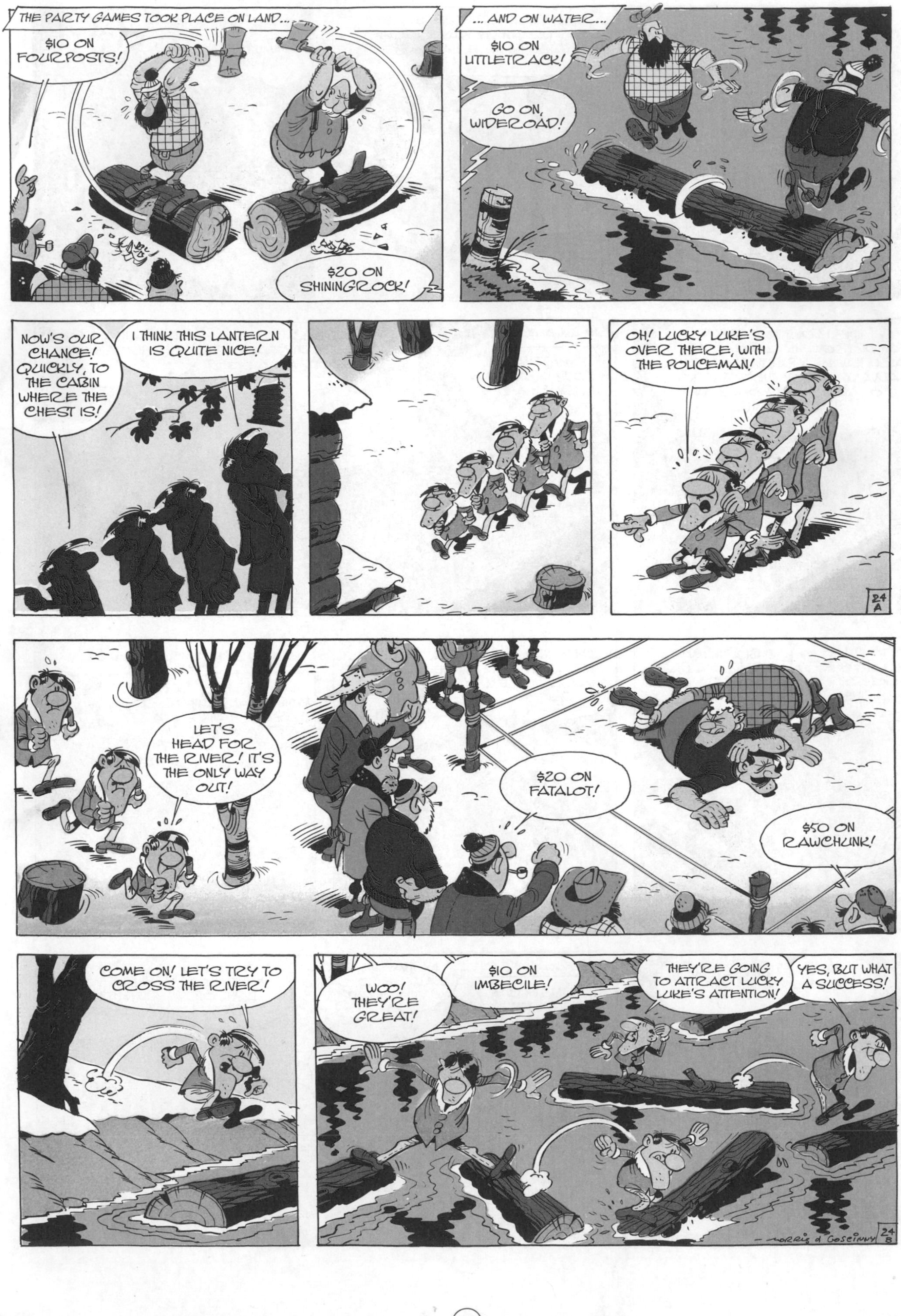
THE PARTY GAMES TOOK PLACE ON LAND...
$10 ON FOURPOSTS!
$20 ON SHININGROCK!
... AND ON WATER...
$10 ON LITTLETRACK!
GO ON, WIDEROAD!
NOW'S OUR CHANCE! QUICKLY, TO THE CABIN WHERE THE CHEST IS!
I THINK THIS LANTERN IS QUITE NICE!
OH! LUCKY LUKE'S OVER THERE, WITH THE POLICEMAN!
24 A
LET'S HEAD FOR THE RIVER! IT'S THE ONLY WAY OUT!
$20 ON FATALOT!
$50 ON RAWCHUNK!
COME ON! LET'S TRY TO CROSS THE RIVER!
WOO! THEY'RE GREAT!
$10 ON IMBECILE!
THEY'RE GOING TO ATTRACT LUCKY LUKE'S ATTENTION!
YES, BUT WHAT A SUCCESS!
24 B

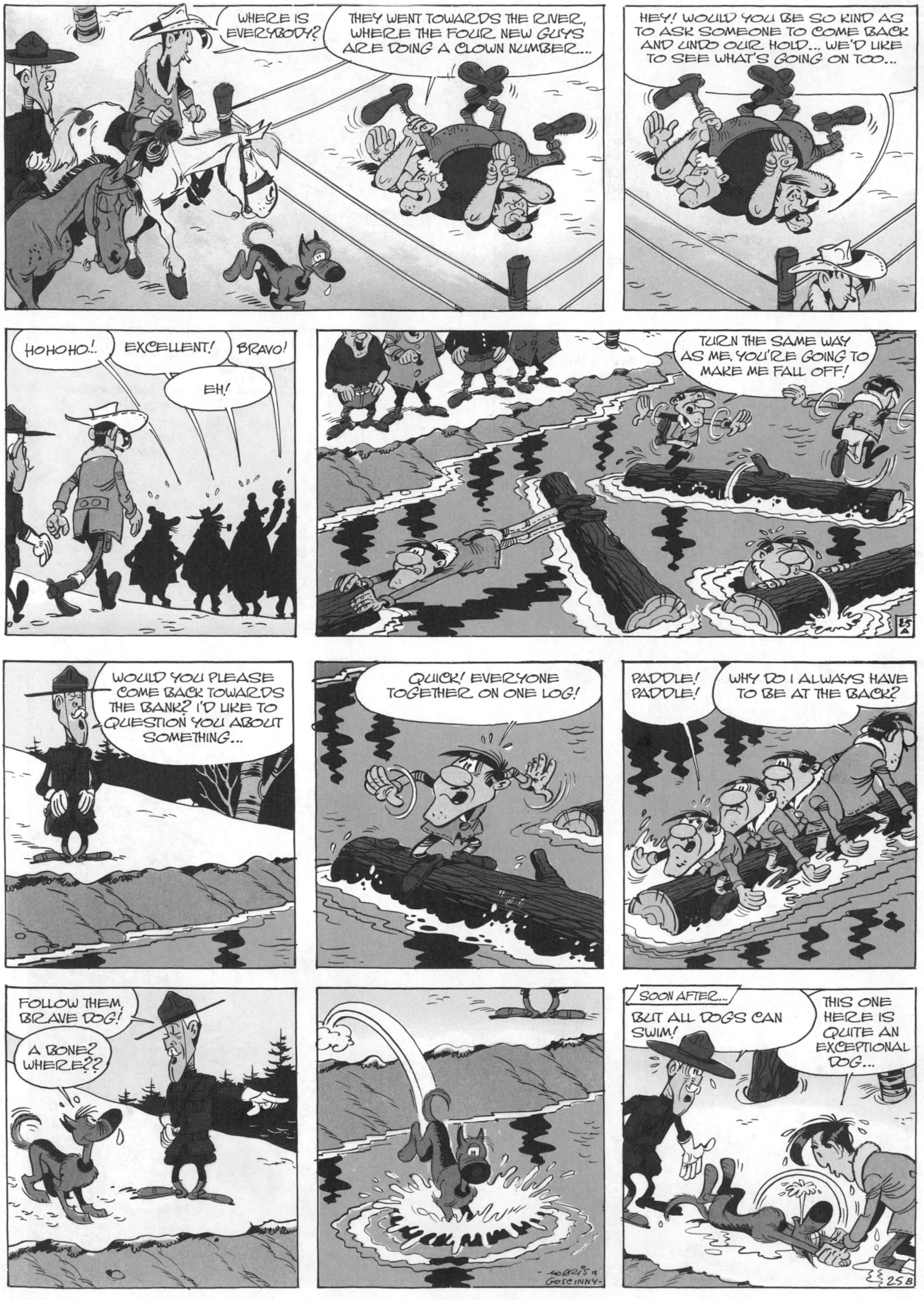
WHERE IS EVERYBODY?
THEY WENT TOWARDS THE RIVER, WHERE THE FOUR NEW GUYS ARE DOING A CLOWN NUMBER...
HEY! WOULD YOU BE SO KIND AS TO ASK SOMEONE TO COME BACK AND UNDO OUR HOLD... WE'D LIKE TO SEE WHAT'S GOING ON TOO...
HOHOHO!..
EXCELLENT!
BRAVO!
EH!
TURN THE SAME WAY AS ME, YOU'RE GOING TO MAKE ME FALL OFF!
WOULD YOU PLEASE COME BACK TOWARDS THE BANK? I'D LIKE TO QUESTION YOU ABOUT SOMETHING...
QUICK! EVERYONE TOGETHER ON ONE LOG!
PADDLE! PADDLE!
WHY DO I ALWAYS HAVE TO BE AT THE BACK?
FOLLOW THEM, BRAVE DOG!
A BONE? WHERE??
SOON AFTER...
BUT ALL DOGS CAN SWIM!
THIS ONE HERE IS QUITE AN EXCEPTIONAL DOG...

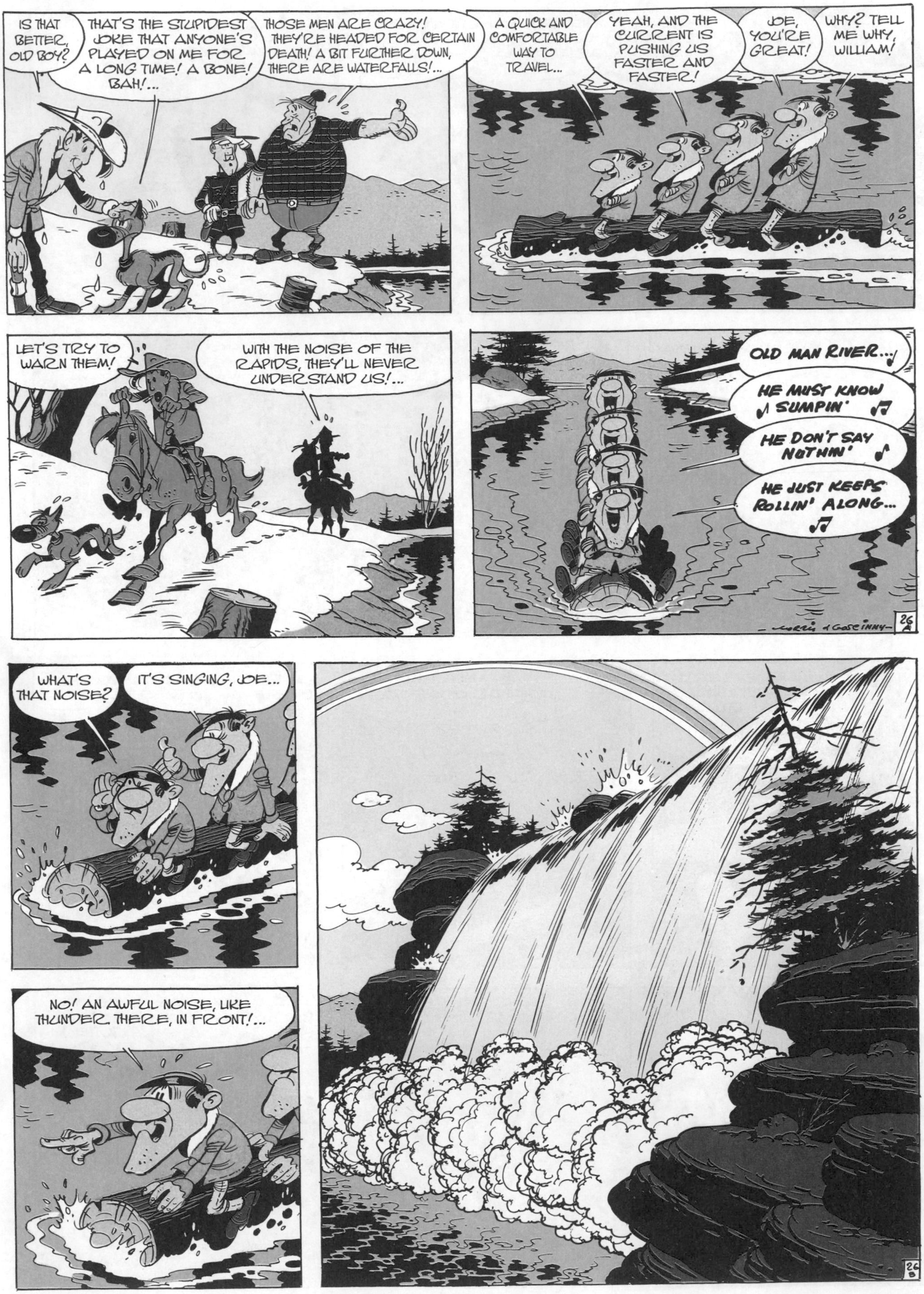
IS THAT BETTER, OLD BOY?
THAT'S THE STUPIDEST JOKE THAT ANYONE'S PLAYED ON ME FOR A LONG TIME! A BONE! BAH!...
THOSE MEN ARE CRAZY! THEY'RE HEADED FOR CERTAIN DEATH! A BIT FURTHER DOWN, THERE ARE WATERFALLS!...
A QUICK AND COMFORTABLE WAY TO TRAVEL...
YEAH, AND THE CURRENT IS PUSHING US FASTER AND FASTER!
JOE, YOU'RE GREAT!
WHY? TELL ME WHY, WILLIAM!
LET'S TRY TO WARN THEM!
WITH THE NOISE OF THE RAPIDS, THEY'LL NEVER UNDERSTAND US!...
OLD MAN RIVER...
HE MUST KNOW SUMPIN'
HE DON'T SAY NUTHIN'
HE JUST KEEPS ROLLIN' ALONG...
26 A
MORRIS & GOSCINNY
WHAT'S THAT NOISE?
IT'S SINGING, JOE...
NO! AN AWFUL NOISE, LIKE THUNDER. THERE, IN FRONT!...
26 B

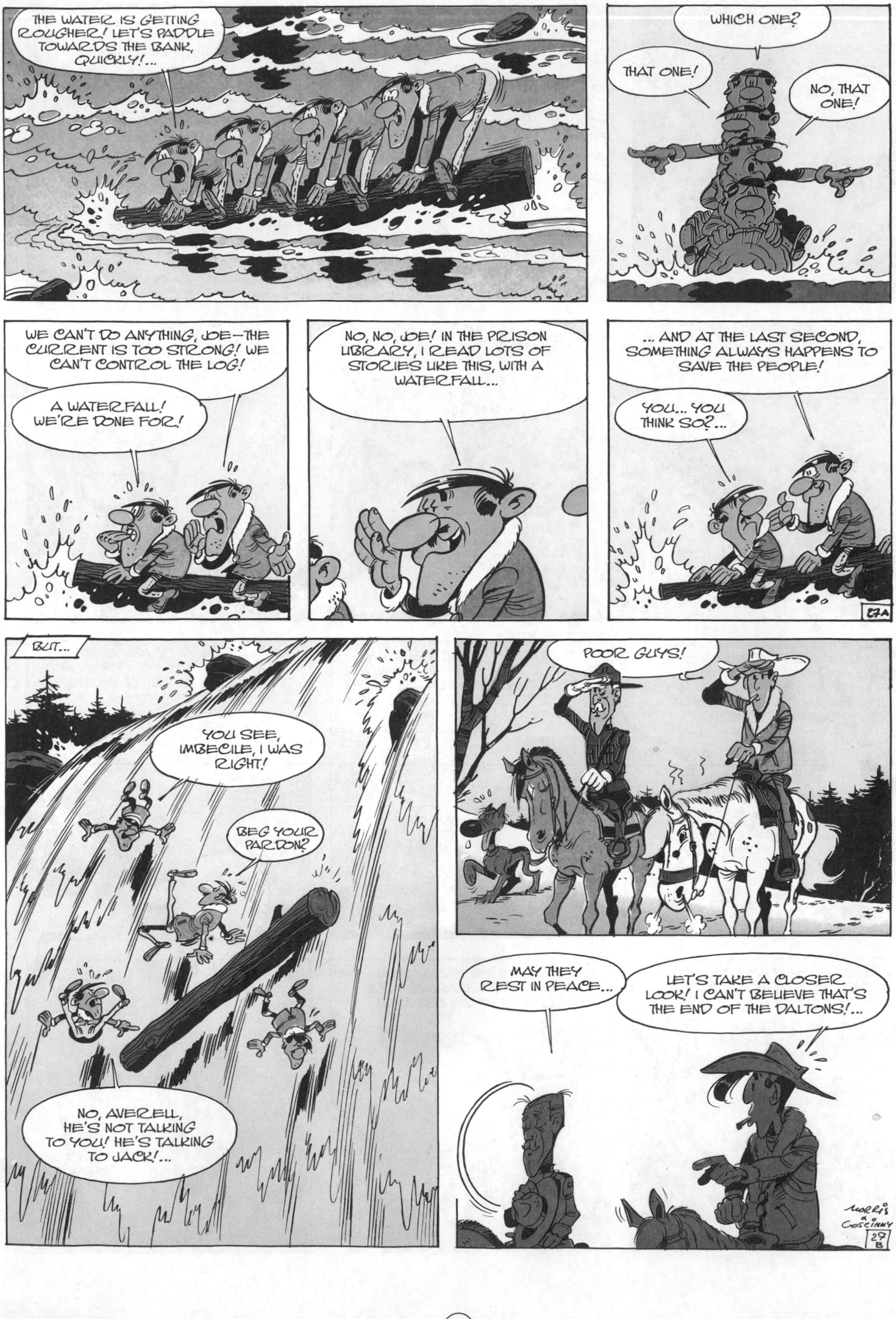
THE WATER IS GETTING ROUGHER! LET'S PADDLE TOWARDS THE BANK, QUICKLY!...
WHICH ONE?
THAT ONE!
NO, THAT ONE!
WE CAN'T DO ANYTHING, JOE—THE CURRENT IS TOO STRONG! WE CAN'T CONTROL THE LOG!
A WATERFALL! WE'RE DONE FOR!
NO, NO, JOE! IN THE PRISON LIBRARY, I READ LOTS OF STORIES LIKE THIS, WITH A WATERFALL...
... AND AT THE LAST SECOND, SOMETHING ALWAYS HAPPENS TO SAVE THE PEOPLE!
YOU... YOU THINK SO?...
27A
BUT...
YOU SEE, IMBECILE, I WAS RIGHT!
BEG YOUR PARDON?
NO, AVERELL, HE'S NOT TALKING TO YOU! HE'S TALKING TO JACK!...
POOR GUYS!
MAY THEY REST IN PEACE...
LET'S TAKE A CLOSER LOOK! I CAN'T BELIEVE THAT'S THE END OF THE DALTONS!...
MORRIS & GOSCINNY
27 B

IT'LL TAKE US THREE OR FOUR HOURS TO REACH THE FOOT OF THE FALLS...

BUT AT THE FOOT OF THE FALLS, STRANGE THINGS WERE HAPPENING...

MAY MY SON PUT THE PALEFACES IN THE SLED. WE'LL TAKE THEM TO OUR TEEPEE...

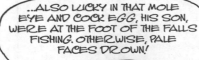

SOON AFTER...

THAT PALEFACE IS STARTING TO STIR...

WE... WE'RE NOT DEAD?

PALEFACES ARE VERY LUCKY TO HAVE ROCK-HARD SCALP THAT WATER CANNOT BREAK...

..ALSO LUCKY IN THAT MOLE EYE AND COCK EGG, HIS SON, WERE AT THE FOOT OF THE FALLS FISHING. OTHERWISE, PALE FACES DROWN!

AH! WHAT DID I TELL YOU?... WITH FALLS, YOU ALWAYS GET AWAY WITH IT!...

YEAH! IN ANY CASE, WE HAVE TO LEAVE RIGHT NOW FOR THE NORTH!

THE PALEFACE IS CRAZY UNDER HIS HARD SCALP. WINTER IS COMING. GOING ON FOOT TO THE NORTH IS IMPOSSIBLE.

OF COURSE, WE NEED A SLED, DOGS, COVERS AND SUPPLIES...

MOLE EYE ONLY HAS ONE SLED, AND HE NEEDS HIS SUPPLIES...

I WONDER IF THE POWDER IN OUR BULLETS IS DRY YET...

OH, THANKS TO THE FIRE'S WARMTH, PALEFACES' WEAPONS ARE READY TO BE USED!...

PERFECT! GIVE US YOUR SLED AND SUPPLIES!

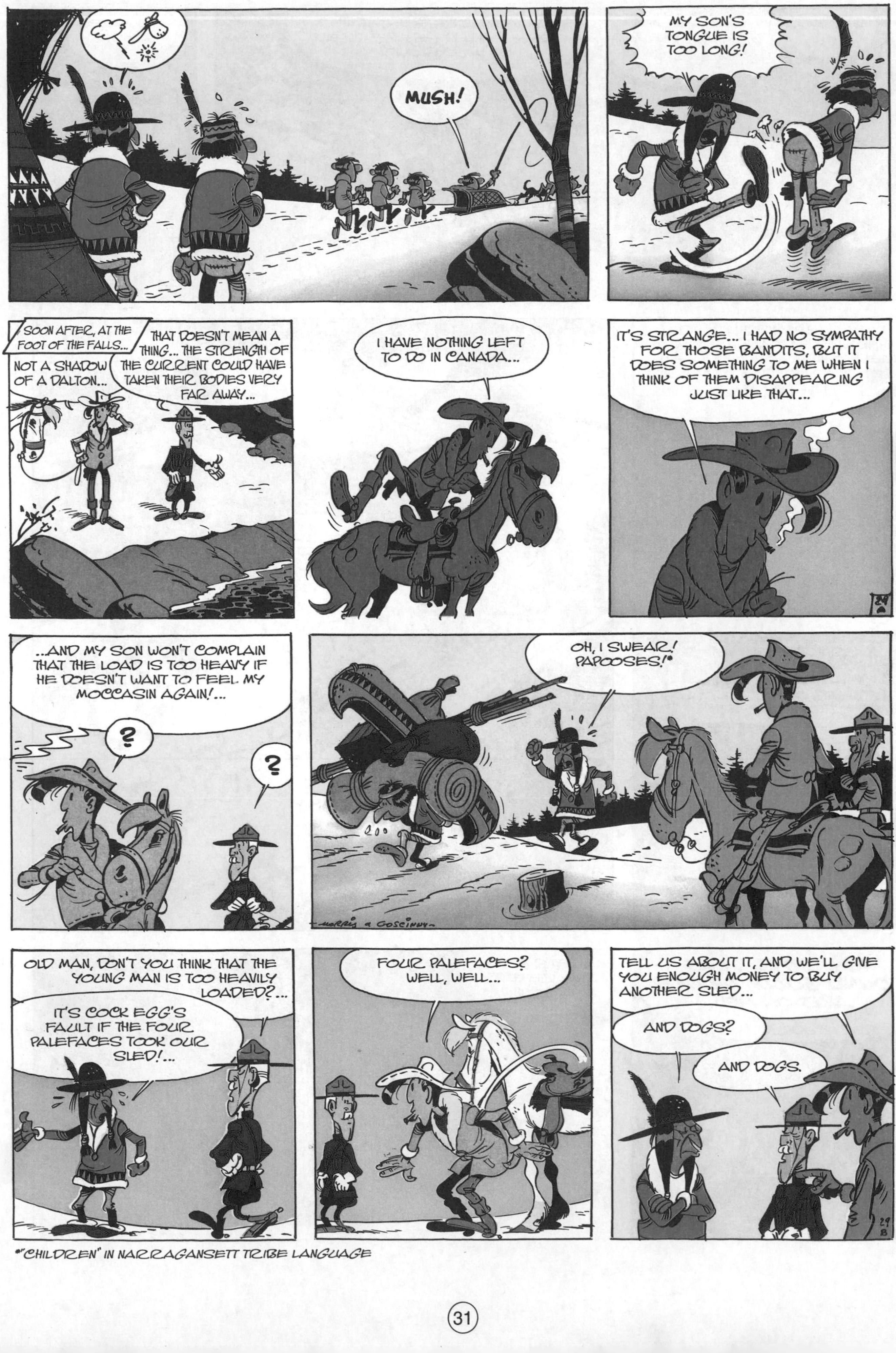
MUSH!
MY SON'S TONGUE IS TOO LONG!
SOON AFTER, AT THE FOOT OF THE FALLS...
NOT A SHADOW OF A DALTON...
THAT DOESN'T MEAN A THING... THE STRENGTH OF THE CURRENT COULD HAVE TAKEN THEIR BODIES VERY FAR AWAY...
I HAVE NOTHING LEFT TO DO IN CANADA...
IT'S STRANGE... I HAD NO SYMPATHY FOR THOSE BANDITS, BUT IT DOES SOMETHING TO ME WHEN I THINK OF THEM DISAPPEARING JUST LIKE THAT...
...AND MY SON WON'T COMPLAIN THAT THE LOAD IS TOO HEAVY IF HE DOESN'T WANT TO FEEL MY MOCCASIN AGAIN!...
?
?
OH, I SWEAR! PAPOOSES!*
MORRIS & GOSCINNY
OLD MAN, DON'T YOU THINK THAT THE YOUNG MAN IS TOO HEAVILY LOADED?...
IT'S COCK EGG'S FAULT IF THE FOUR PALEFACES TOOK OUR SLED!...
FOUR PALEFACES? WELL, WELL...
TELL US ABOUT IT, AND WE'LL GIVE YOU ENOUGH MONEY TO BUY ANOTHER SLED...
AND DOGS?
AND DOGS.

*"CHILDREN" IN NARRAGANSETT TRIBE LANGUAGE

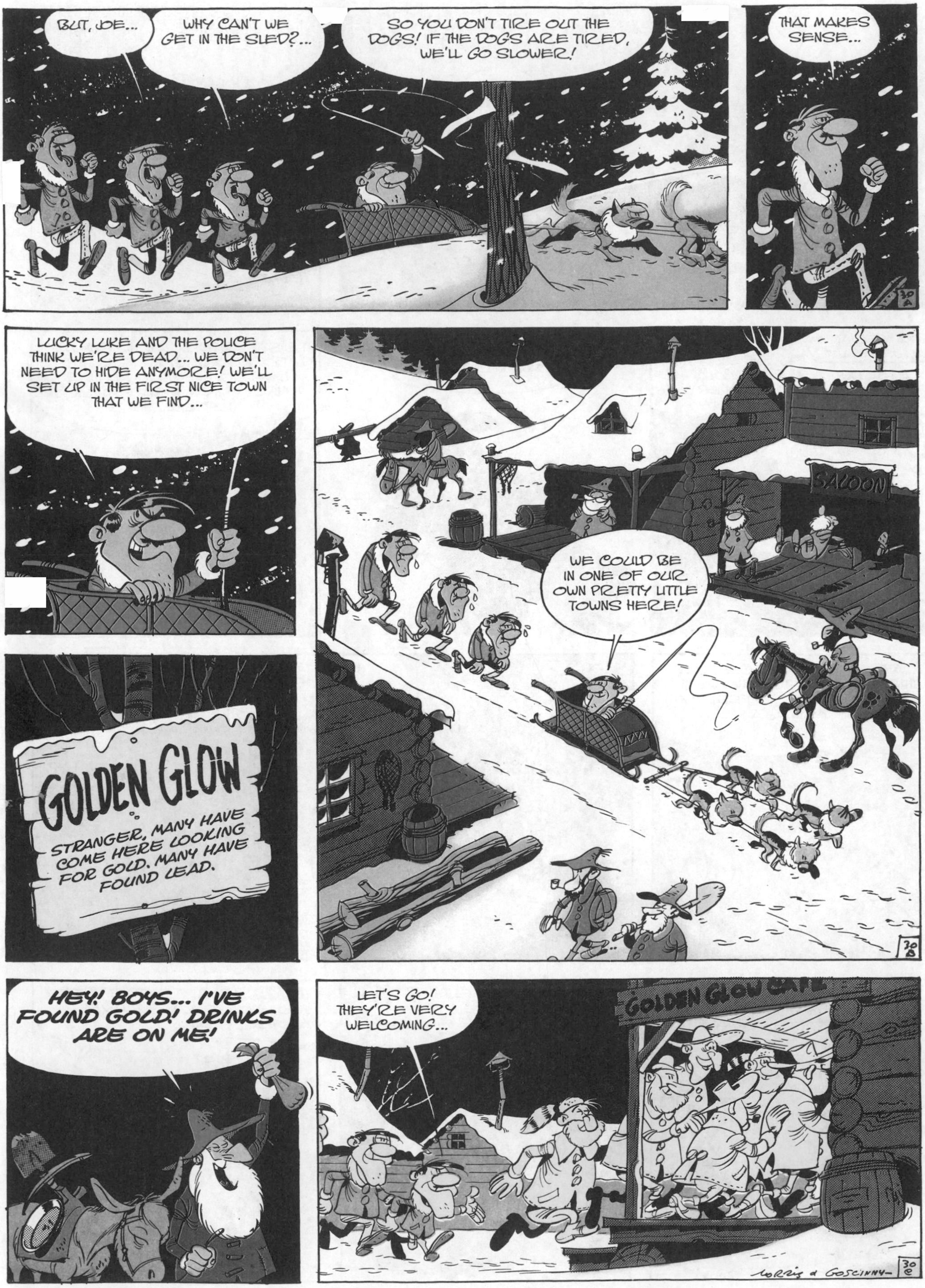

BUT, JOE...
WHY CAN'T WE GET IN THE SLED?...
SO YOU DON'T TIRE OUT THE DOGS! IF THE DOGS ARE TIRED, WE'LL GO SLOWER!
THAT MAKES SENSE...
LUCKY LUKE AND THE POLICE THINK WE'RE DEAD... WE DON'T NEED TO HIDE ANYMORE! WE'LL SET UP IN THE FIRST NICE TOWN THAT WE FIND...
SALOON
WE COULD BE IN ONE OF OUR OWN PRETTY LITTLE TOWNS HERE!
GOLDEN GLOW
STRANGER, MANY HAVE COME HERE LOOKING FOR GOLD. MANY HAVE FOUND LEAD.
HEY! BOYS... I'VE FOUND GOLD! DRINKS ARE ON ME!
LET'S GO! THEY'RE VERY WELCOMING...
GOLDEN GLOW CAFE

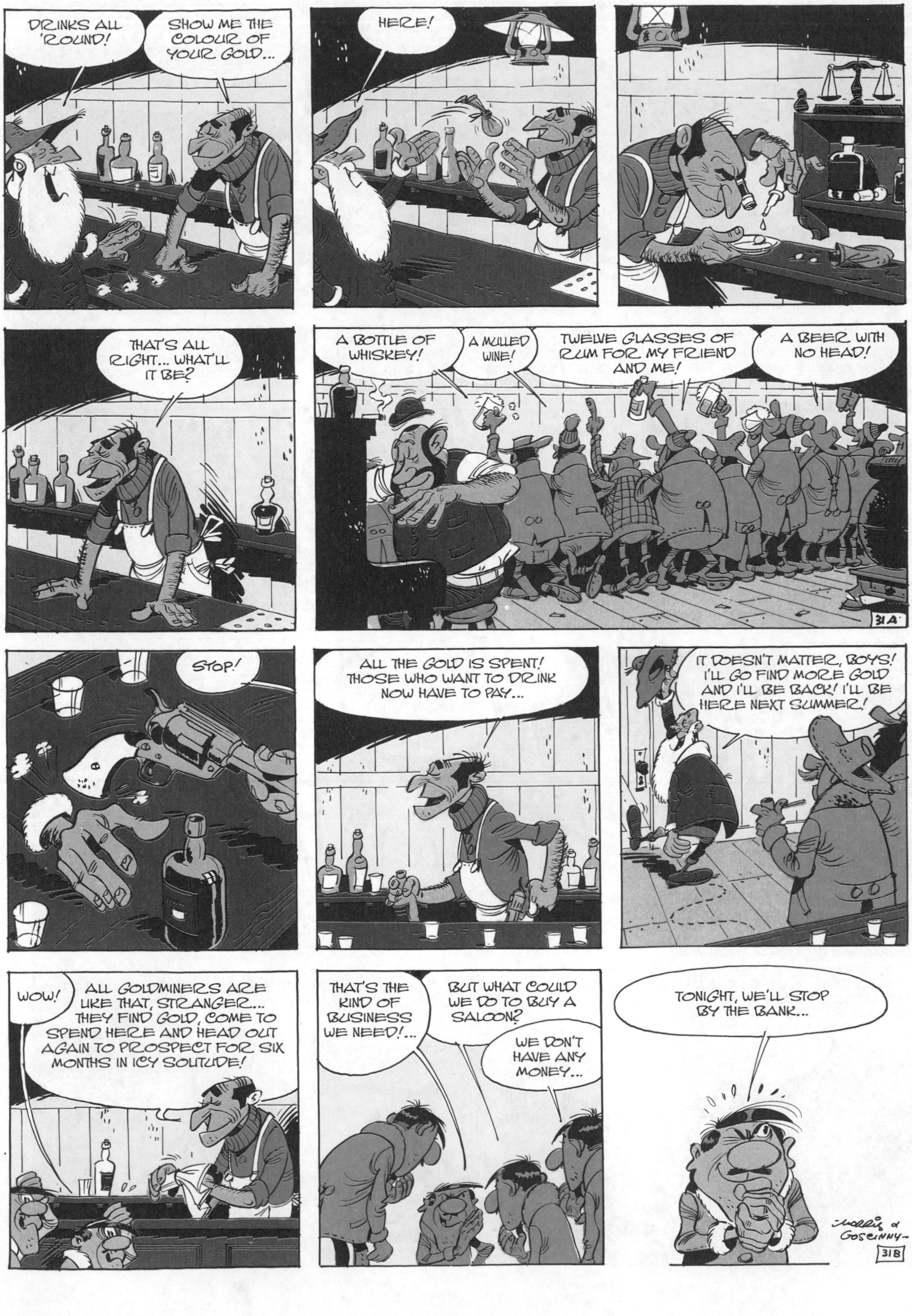
DRINKS ALL 'ROUND!
SHOW ME THE COLOUR OF YOUR GOLD...
HERE!
THAT'S ALL RIGHT... WHAT'LL IT BE?
A BOTTLE OF WHISKEY!
A MULLED WINE!
TWELVE GLASSES OF RUM FOR MY FRIEND AND ME!
A BEER WITH NO HEAD!
31A
STOP!
ALL THE GOLD IS SPENT! THOSE WHO WANT TO DRINK NOW HAVE TO PAY...
IT DOESN'T MATTER, BOYS! I'LL GO FIND MORE GOLD AND I'LL BE BACK! I'LL BE HERE NEXT SUMMER!
WOW!
ALL GOLDMINERS ARE LIKE THAT, STRANGER... THEY FIND GOLD, COME TO SPEND HERE AND HEAD OUT AGAIN TO PROSPECT FOR SIX MONTHS IN ICY SOLITUDE!
THAT'S THE KIND OF BUSINESS WE NEED!...
BUT WHAT COULD WE DO TO BUY A SALOON?
WE DON'T HAVE ANY MONEY...
TONIGHT, WE'LL STOP BY THE BANK...
MORRIS & GOSCINNY
31B

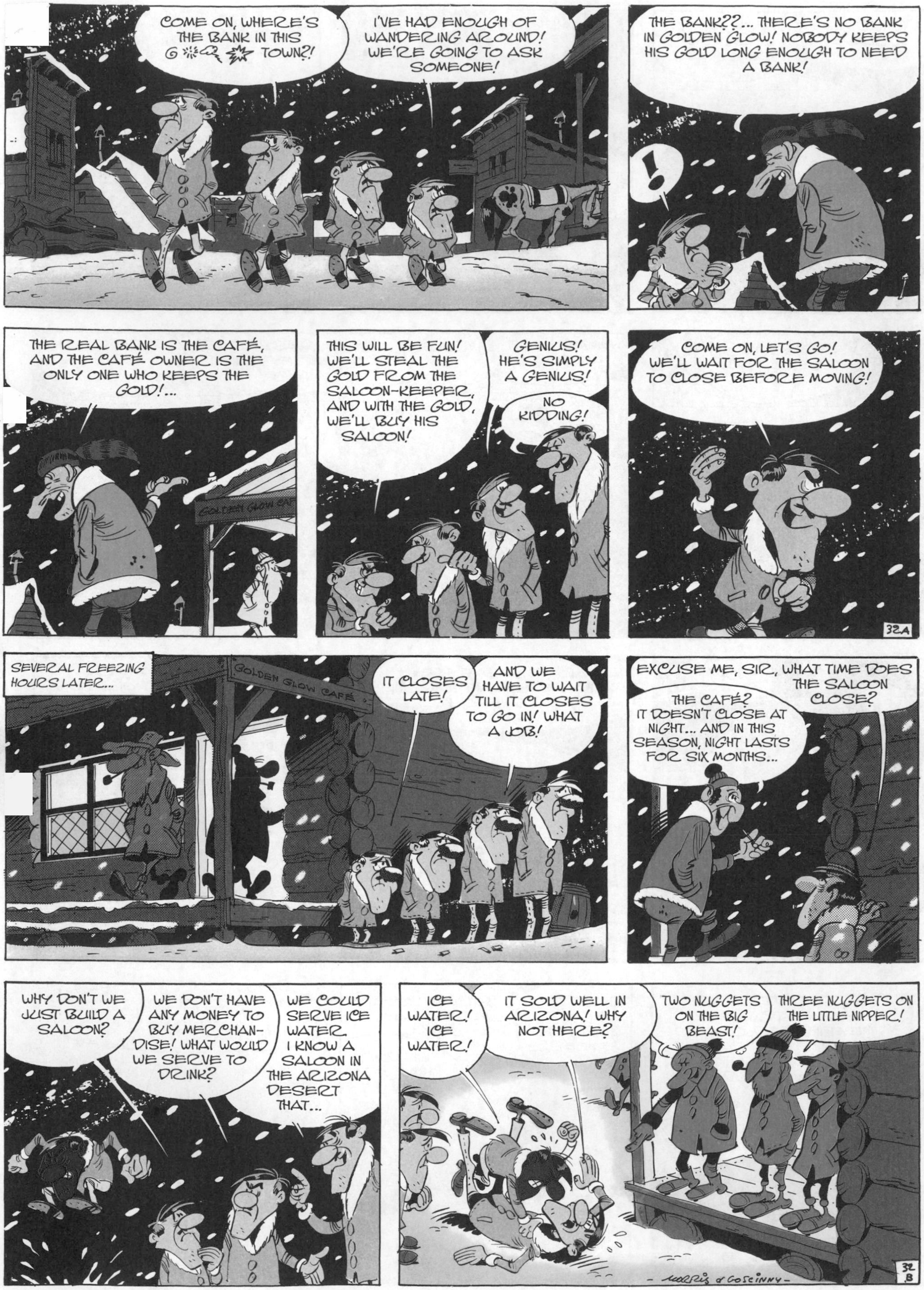
COME ON, WHERE'S THE BANK IN THIS TOWN?!
I'VE HAD ENOUGH OF WANDERING AROUND! WE'RE GOING TO ASK SOMEONE!
THE BANK??... THERE'S NO BANK IN GOLDEN GLOW! NOBODY KEEPS HIS GOLD LONG ENOUGH TO NEED A BANK!
!
THE REAL BANK IS THE CAFÉ, AND THE CAFÉ OWNER IS THE ONLY ONE WHO KEEPS THE GOLD!...
THIS WILL BE FUN! WE'LL STEAL THE GOLD FROM THE SALOON-KEEPER, AND WITH THE GOLD, WE'LL BUY HIS SALOON!
GENIUS! HE'S SIMPLY A GENIUS!
NO KIDDING!
COME ON, LET'S GO! WE'LL WAIT FOR THE SALOON TO CLOSE BEFORE MOVING!
32A
SEVERAL FREEZING HOURS LATER...
GOLDEN GLOW CAFÉ
IT CLOSES LATE!
AND WE HAVE TO WAIT TILL IT CLOSES TO GO IN! WHAT A JOB!
EXCUSE ME, SIR, WHAT TIME DOES THE SALOON CLOSE?
THE CAFÉ? IT DOESN'T CLOSE AT NIGHT... AND IN THIS SEASON, NIGHT LASTS FOR SIX MONTHS...
WHY DON'T WE JUST BUILD A SALOON?
WE DON'T HAVE ANY MONEY TO BUY MERCHANDISE! WHAT WOULD WE SERVE TO DRINK?
WE COULD SERVE ICE WATER. I KNOW A SALOON IN THE ARIZONA DESERT THAT...
ICE WATER! ICE WATER!
IT SOLD WELL IN ARIZONA! WHY NOT HERE?
TWO NUGGETS ON THE BIG BEAST!
THREE NUGGETS ON THE LITTLE NIPPER!
32 B
- MORRIS & GOSCINNY -

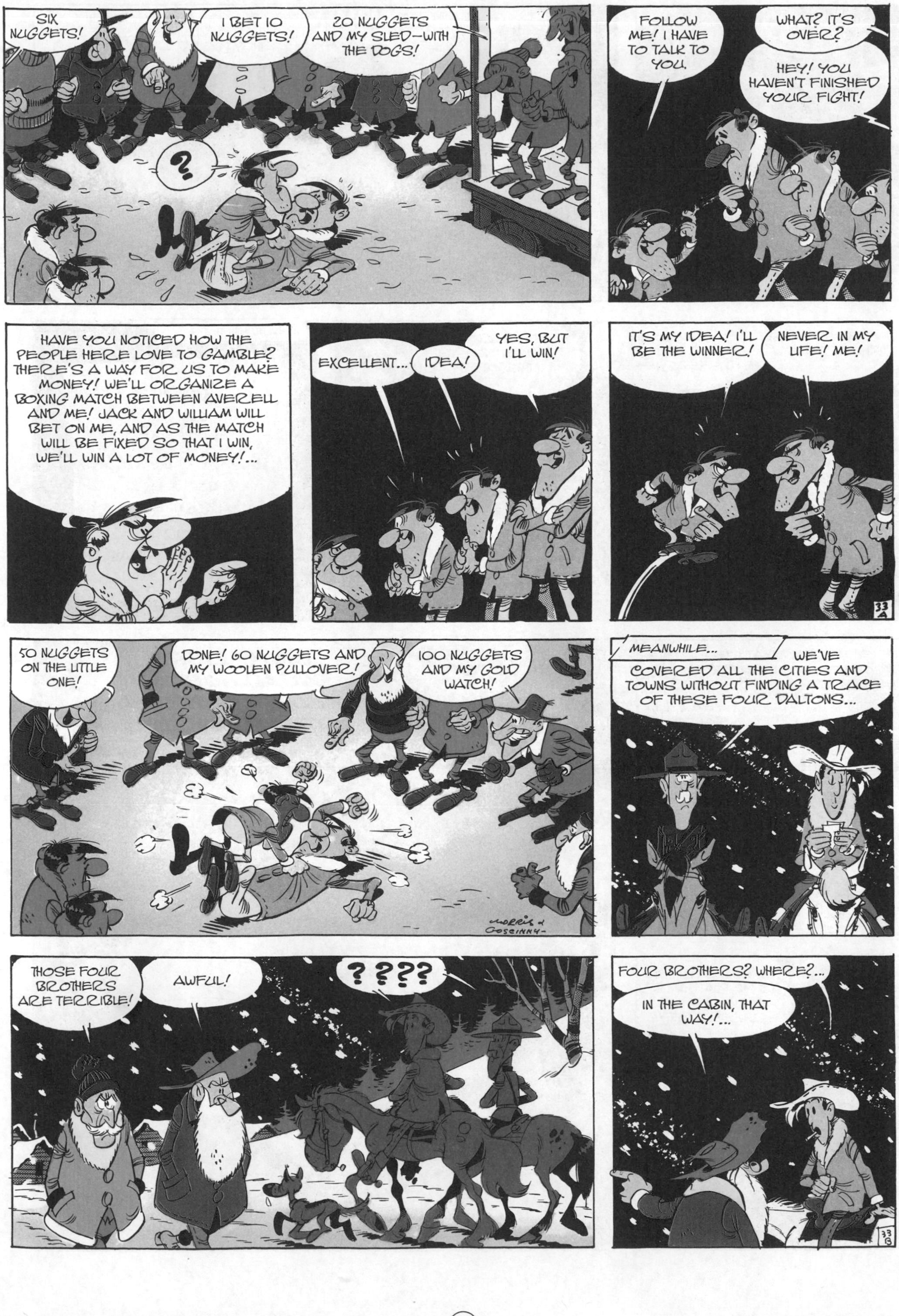

SIX NUGGETS!
I BET 10 NUGGETS!
20 NUGGETS AND MY SLED—WITH THE DOGS!
?
FOLLOW ME! I HAVE TO TALK TO YOU.
WHAT? IT'S OVER?
HEY! YOU HAVEN'T FINISHED YOUR FIGHT!
HAVE YOU NOTICED HOW THE PEOPLE HERE LOVE TO GAMBLE? THERE'S A WAY FOR US TO MAKE MONEY! WE'LL ORGANIZE A BOXING MATCH BETWEEN AVERELL AND ME! JACK AND WILLIAM WILL BET ON ME, AND AS THE MATCH WILL BE FIXED SO THAT I WIN, WE'LL WIN A LOT OF MONEY!...
EXCELLENT...
IDEA!
YES, BUT I'LL WIN!
IT'S MY IDEA! I'LL BE THE WINNER!
NEVER IN MY LIFE! ME!
33 A
50 NUGGETS ON THE LITTLE ONE!
DONE! 60 NUGGETS AND MY WOOLEN PULLOVER!
100 NUGGETS AND MY GOLD WATCH!
MORRIS & GOSCINNY
MEANWHILE...
WE'VE COVERED ALL THE CITIES AND TOWNS WITHOUT FINDING A TRACE OF THESE FOUR DALTONS...
THOSE FOUR BROTHERS ARE TERRIBLE!
AWFUL!
????
FOUR BROTHERS? WHERE?...
IN THE CABIN, THAT WAY!...
33 B

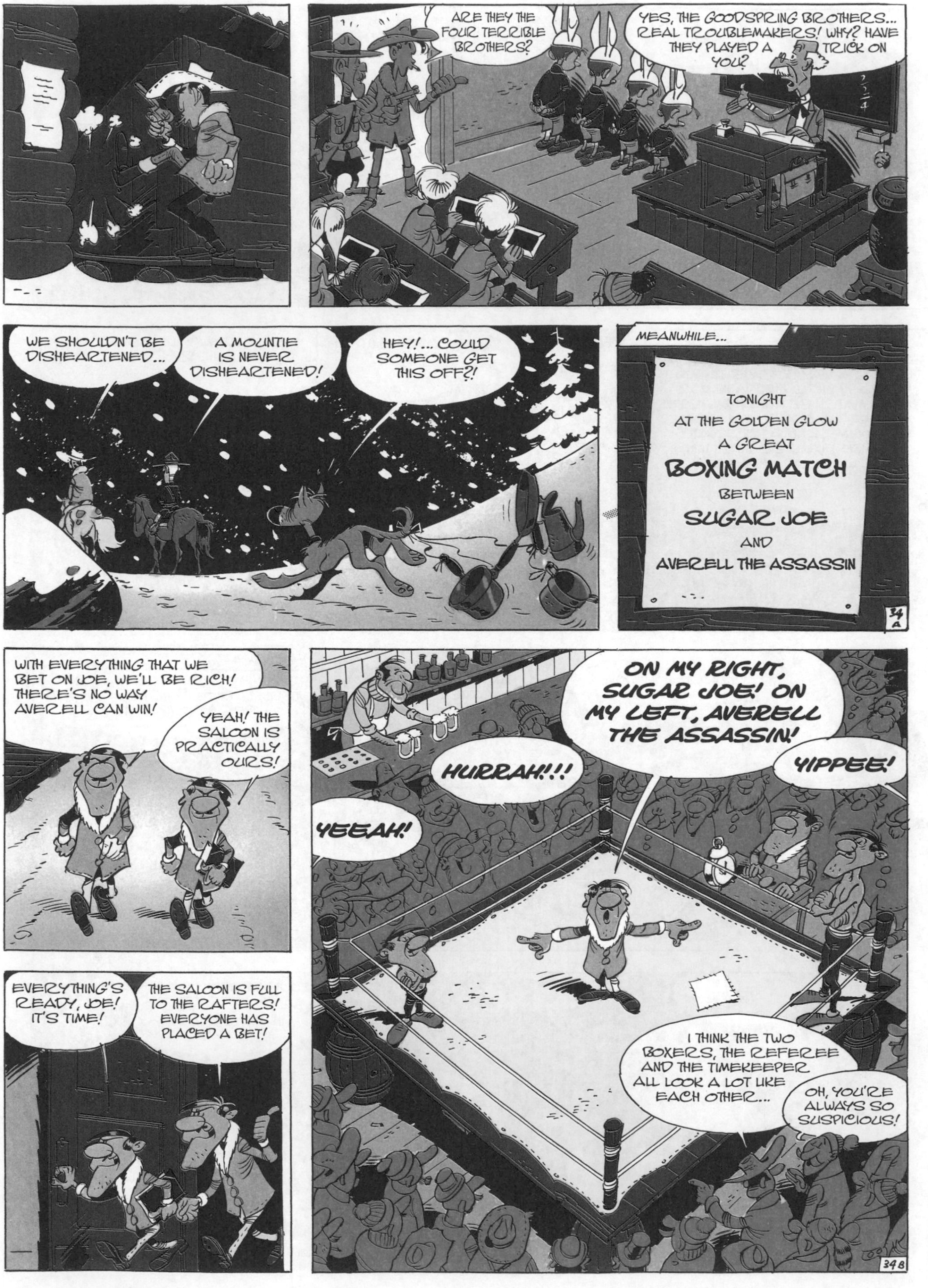
ARE THEY THE FOUR TERRIBLE BROTHERS?
YES, THE GOODSPRING BROTHERS... REAL TROUBLEMAKERS! WHY? HAVE THEY PLAYED A TRICK ON YOU?
WE SHOULDN'T BE DISHEARTENED...
A MOUNTIE IS NEVER DISHEARTENED!
HEY!... COULD SOMEONE GET THIS OFF?!
MEANWHILE...
TONIGHT
AT THE GOLDEN GLOW
A GREAT
BOXING MATCH
BETWEEN
SUGAR JOE
AND
AVERELL THE ASSASSIN
34 A
WITH EVERYTHING THAT WE BET ON JOE, WE'LL BE RICH! THERE'S NO WAY AVERELL CAN WIN!
YEAH! THE SALOON IS PRACTICALLY OURS!
EVERYTHING'S READY, JOE! IT'S TIME!
THE SALOON IS FULL TO THE RAFTERS! EVERYONE HAS PLACED A BET!
ON MY RIGHT, SUGAR JOE! ON MY LEFT, AVERELL THE ASSASSIN!
HURRAH!!!
YIPPEE!
YEEAH!
I THINK THE TWO BOXERS, THE REFEREE AND THE TIMEKEEPER ALL LOOK A LOT LIKE EACH OTHER...
OH, YOU'RE ALWAYS SO SUSPICIOUS!
34 B

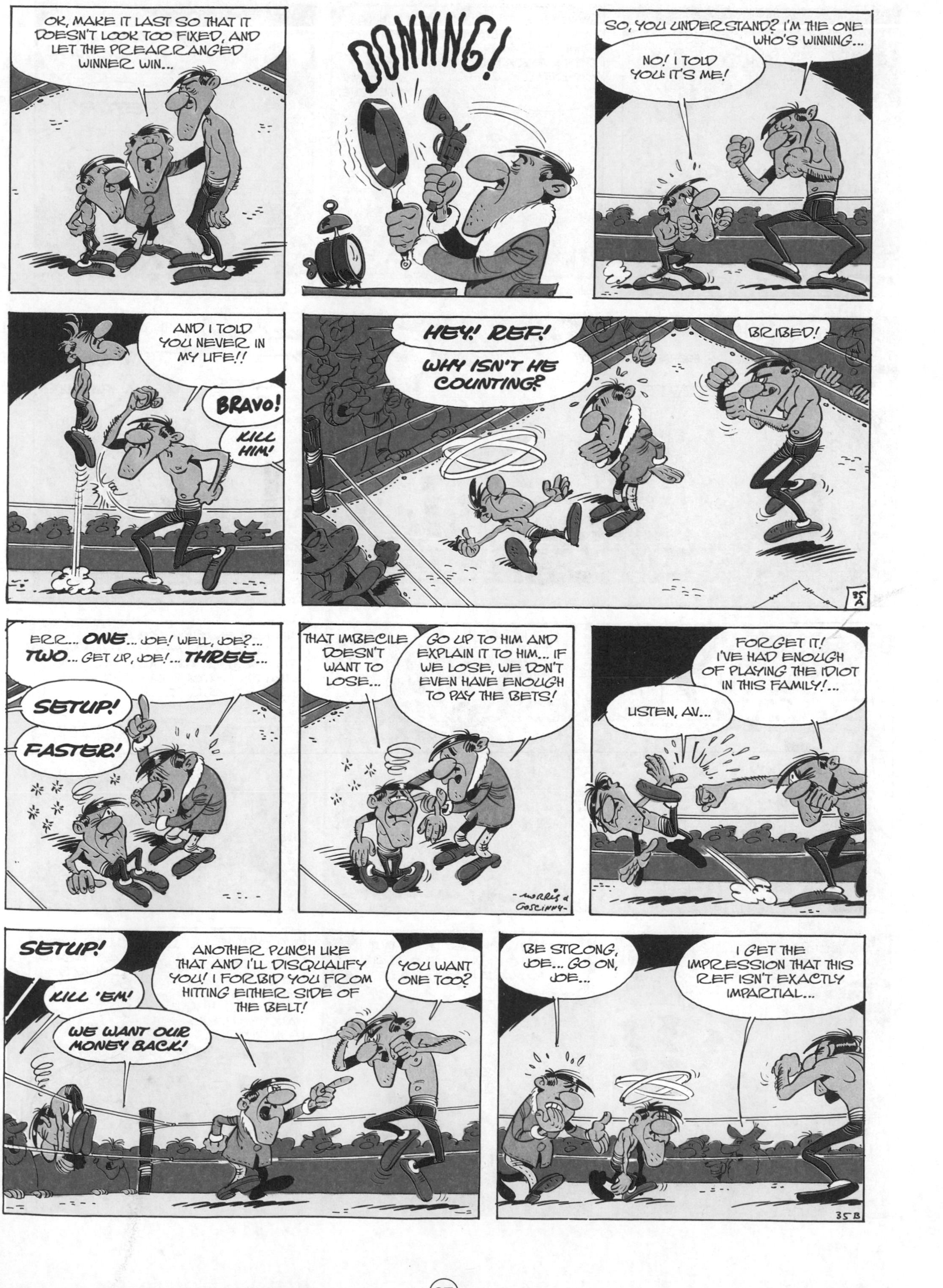
OK, MAKE IT LAST SO THAT IT DOESN'T LOOK TOO FIXED, AND LET THE PREARRANGED WINNER WIN...
DONNNG!
SO, YOU UNDERSTAND? I'M THE ONE WHO'S WINNING...
NO! I TOLD YOU: IT'S ME!
AND I TOLD YOU NEVER IN MY LIFE!!
BRAVO!
KILL HIM!
HEY! REF!
WHY ISN'T HE COUNTING?
BRIBED!
ERR... ONE... JOE! WELL, JOE?... TWO... GET UP, JOE!... THREE...
SETUP!
FASTER!
THAT IMBECILE DOESN'T WANT TO LOSE...
GO UP TO HIM AND EXPLAIN IT TO HIM... IF WE LOSE, WE DON'T EVEN HAVE ENOUGH TO PAY THE BETS!
FORGET IT! I'VE HAD ENOUGH OF PLAYING THE IDIOT IN THIS FAMILY!...
LISTEN, AV...
SETUP!
KILL 'EM!
WE WANT OUR MONEY BACK!
ANOTHER PUNCH LIKE THAT AND I'LL DISQUALIFY YOU! I FORBID YOU FROM HITTING EITHER SIDE OF THE BELT!
YOU WANT ONE TOO?
BE STRONG, JOE... GO ON, JOE...
I GET THE IMPRESSION THAT THIS REF ISN'T EXACTLY IMPARTIAL...

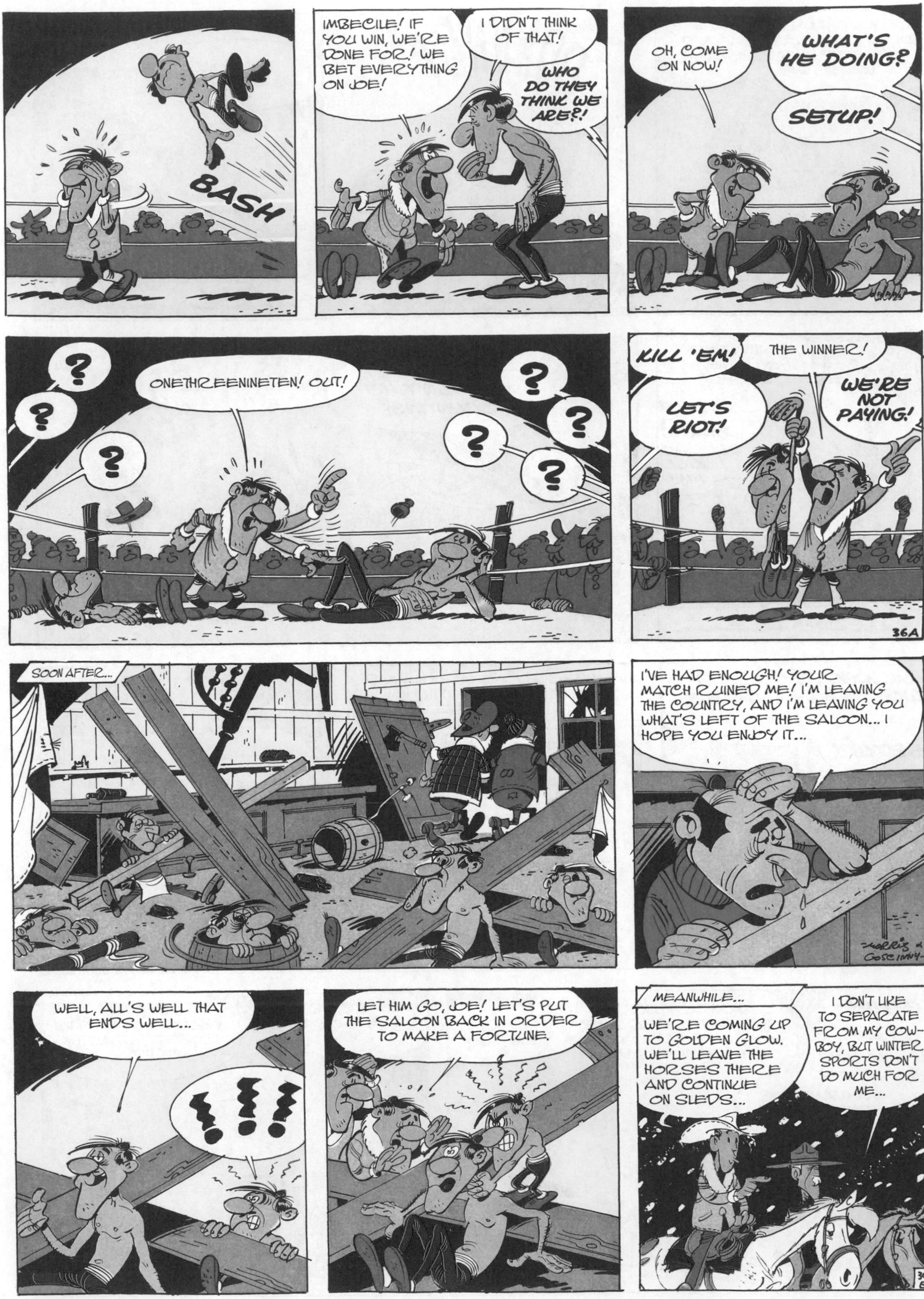

BASH
IMBECILE! IF YOU WIN, WE'RE DONE FOR! WE BET EVERYTHING ON JOE!
I DIDN'T THINK OF THAT!
WHO DO THEY THINK WE ARE?!
OH, COME ON NOW!
WHAT'S HE DOING?
SETUP!
?
?
?
ONETHREENINETEN! OUT!
?
?
?
KILL 'EM!
THE WINNER!
LET'S RIOT!
WE'RE NOT PAYING!
36A
SOON AFTER...
I'VE HAD ENOUGH! YOUR MATCH RUINED ME! I'M LEAVING THE COUNTRY, AND I'M LEAVING YOU WHAT'S LEFT OF THE SALOON... I HOPE YOU ENJOY IT...
WELL, ALL'S WELL THAT ENDS WELL...
!!!
LET HIM GO, JOE! LET'S PUT THE SALOON BACK IN ORDER TO MAKE A FORTUNE.
MEANWHILE...
WE'RE COMING UP TO GOLDEN GLOW. WE'LL LEAVE THE HORSES THERE AND CONTINUE ON SLEDS...
I DON'T LIKE TO SEPARATE FROM MY COWBOY, BUT WINTER SPORTS DON'T DO MUCH FOR ME...

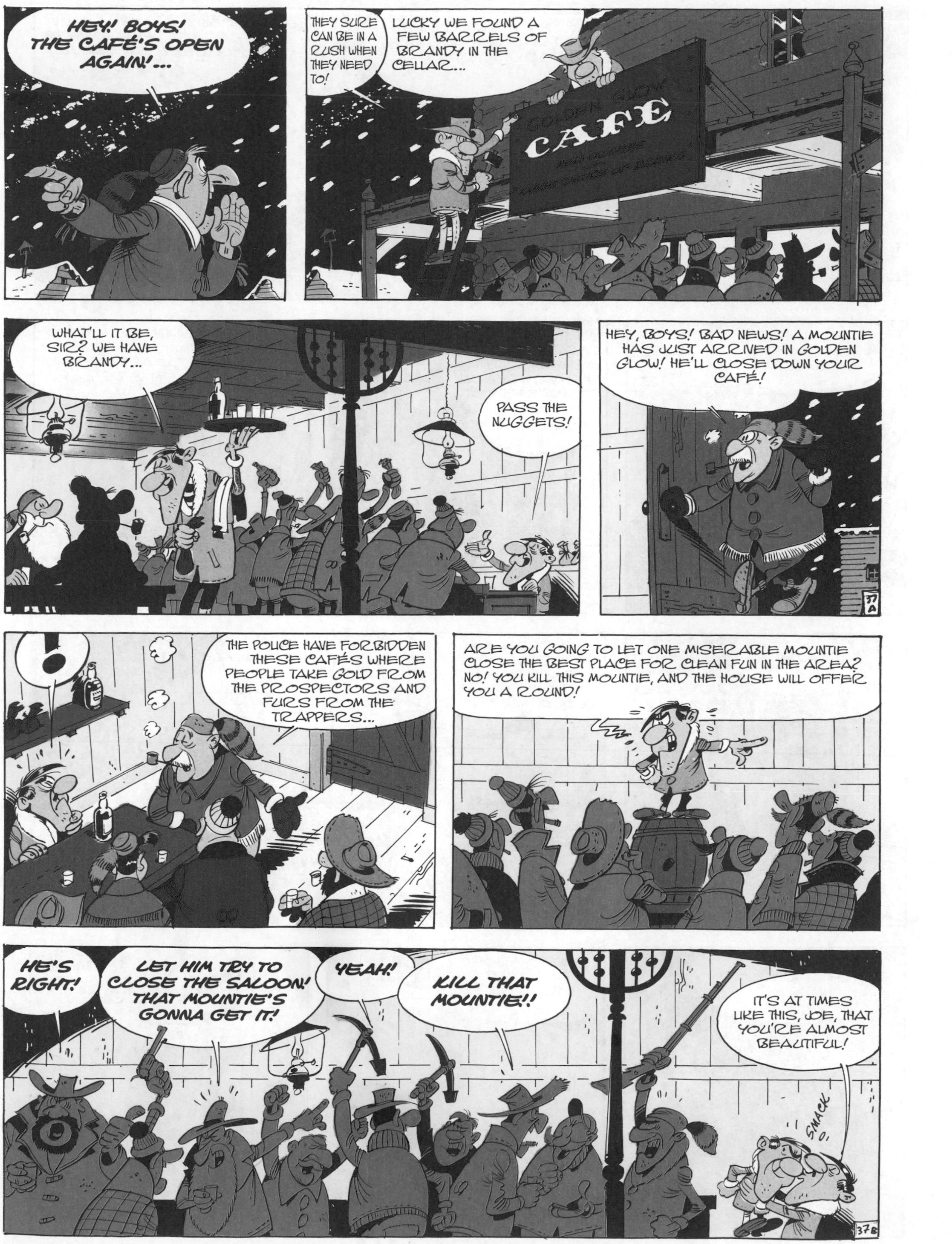
HEY! BOYS! THE CAFÉ'S OPEN AGAIN!...
THEY SURE CAN BE IN A RUSH WHEN THEY NEED TO!
LUCKY WE FOUND A FEW BARRELS OF BRANDY IN THE CELLAR...
CAFE
WHAT'LL IT BE, SIR? WE HAVE BRANDY...
PASS THE NUGGETS!
HEY, BOYS! BAD NEWS! A MOUNTIE HAS JUST ARRIVED IN GOLDEN GLOW! HE'LL CLOSE DOWN YOUR CAFÉ!
!
THE POLICE HAVE FORBIDDEN THESE CAFÉS WHERE PEOPLE TAKE GOLD FROM THE PROSPECTORS AND FURS FROM THE TRAPPERS...
ARE YOU GOING TO LET ONE MISERABLE MOUNTIE CLOSE THE BEST PLACE FOR CLEAN FUN IN THE AREA? NO! YOU KILL THIS MOUNTIE, AND THE HOUSE WILL OFFER YOU A ROUND!
HE'S RIGHT!
LET HIM TRY TO CLOSE THE SALOON! THAT MOUNTIE'S GONNA GET IT!
YEAH!
KILL THAT MOUNTIE!!
IT'S AT TIMES LIKE THIS, JOE, THAT YOU'RE ALMOST BEAUTIFUL!
SMACK

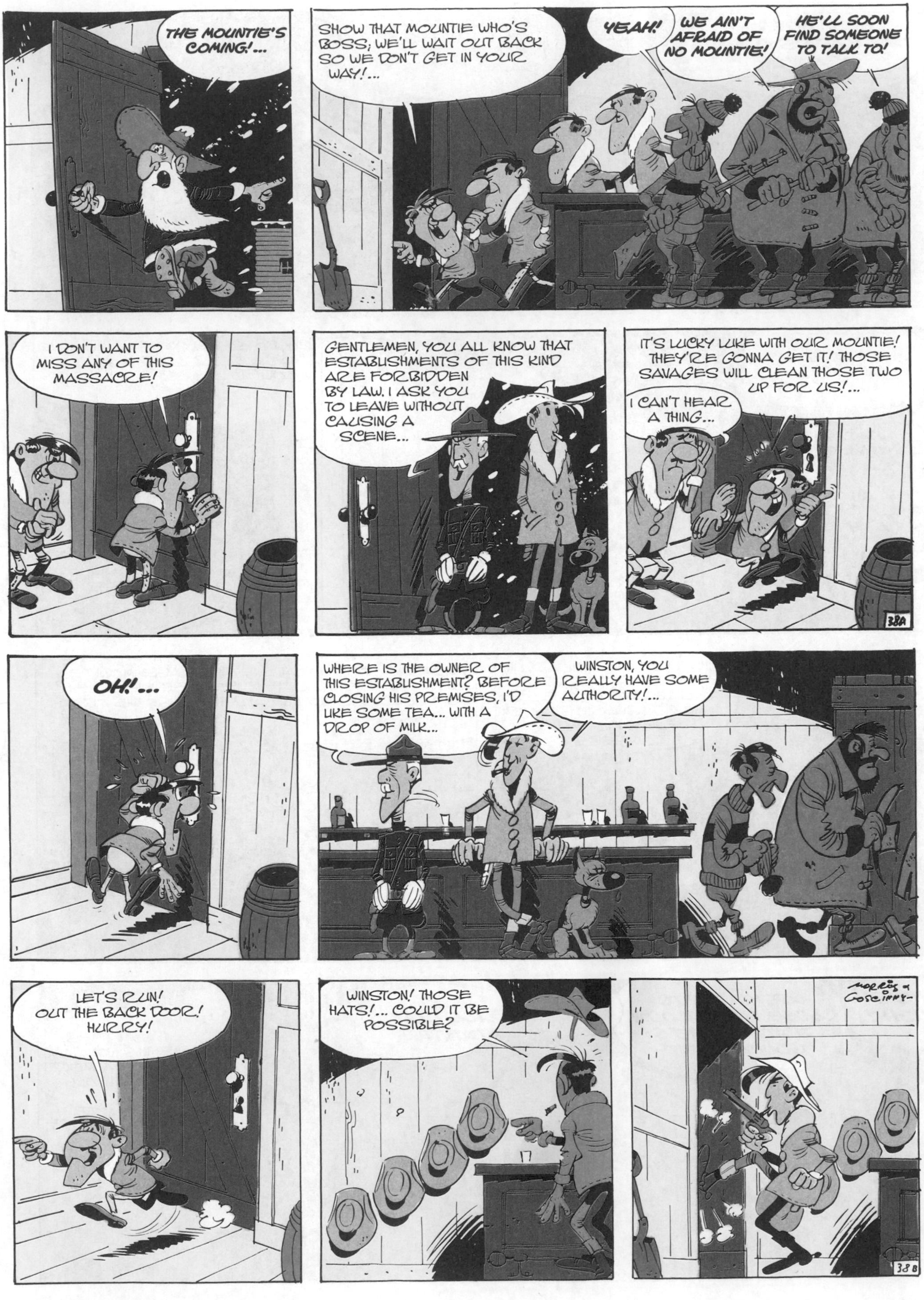
THE MOUNTIE'S COMING!...
SHOW THAT MOUNTIE WHO'S BOSS; WE'LL WAIT OUT BACK SO WE DON'T GET IN YOUR WAY!...
YEAH!
WE AIN'T AFRAID OF NO MOUNTIE!
HE'LL SOON FIND SOMEONE TO TALK TO!
I DON'T WANT TO MISS ANY OF THIS MASSACRE!
GENTLEMEN, YOU ALL KNOW THAT ESTABLISHMENTS OF THIS KIND ARE FORBIDDEN BY LAW. I ASK YOU TO LEAVE WITHOUT CAUSING A SCENE...
IT'S LUCKY LUKE WITH OUR MOUNTIE! THEY'RE GONNA GET IT! THOSE SAVAGES WILL CLEAN THOSE TWO UP FOR US!...
I CAN'T HEAR A THING...
38A
OH!...
WHERE IS THE OWNER OF THIS ESTABLISHMENT? BEFORE CLOSING HIS PREMISES, I'D LIKE SOME TEA... WITH A DROP OF MILK...
WINSTON, YOU REALLY HAVE SOME AUTHORITY!...
LET'S RUN! OUT THE BACK DOOR! HURRY!
WINSTON! THOSE HATS!... COULD IT BE POSSIBLE?
38B

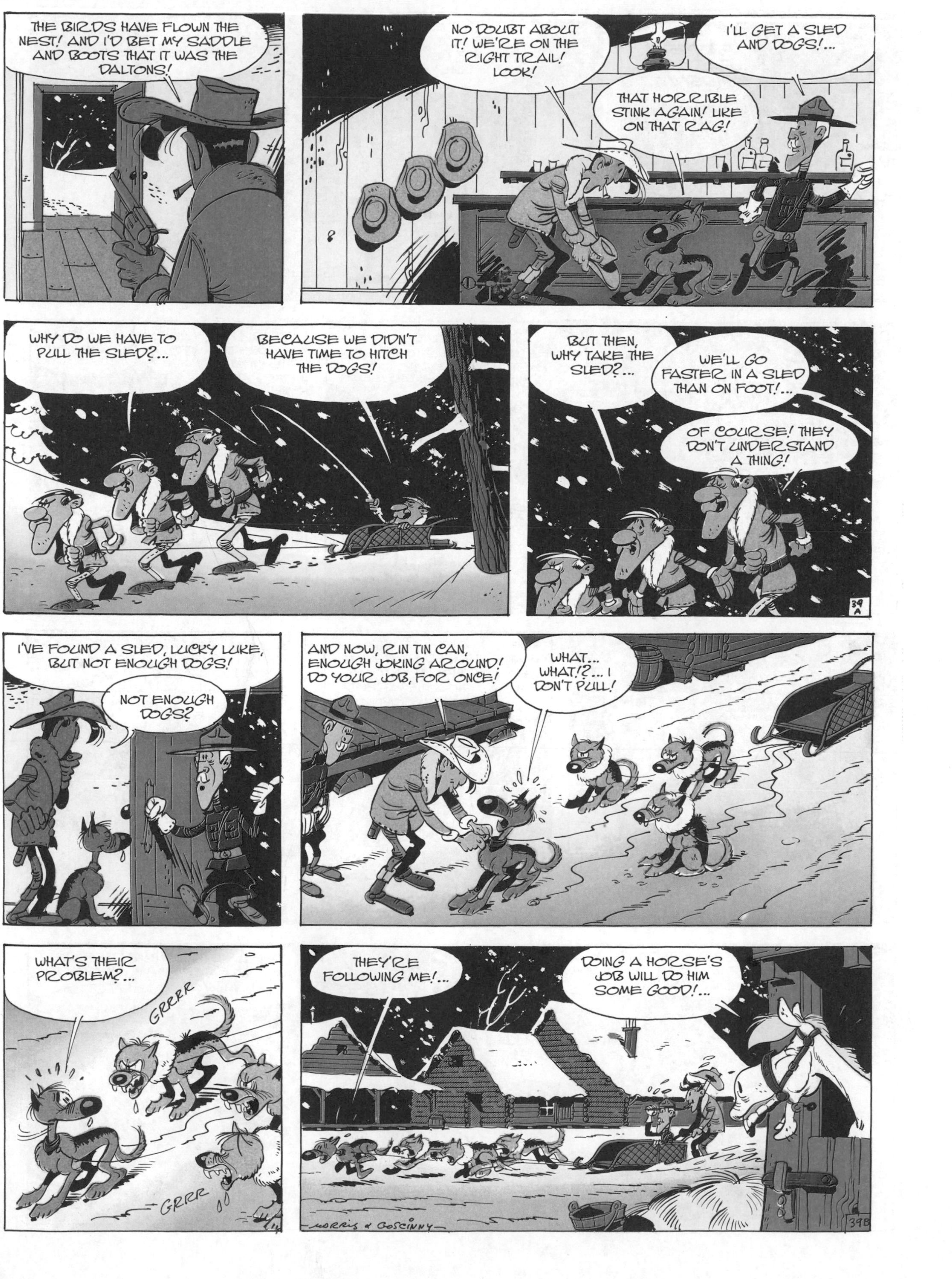
THE BIRDS HAVE FLOWN THE NEST! AND I'D BET MY SADDLE AND BOOTS THAT IT WAS THE DALTONS!
NO DOUBT ABOUT IT! WE'RE ON THE RIGHT TRAIL! LOOK!
THAT HORRIBLE STINK AGAIN! LIKE ON THAT RAG!
I'LL GET A SLED AND DOGS!...
WHY DO WE HAVE TO PULL THE SLED?...
BECAUSE WE DIDN'T HAVE TIME TO HITCH THE DOGS!
BUT THEN, WHY TAKE THE SLED?...
WE'LL GO FASTER IN A SLED THAN ON FOOT!...
OF COURSE! THEY DON'T UNDERSTAND A THING!
39 A
I'VE FOUND A SLED, LUCKY LUKE, BUT NOT ENOUGH DOGS!
NOT ENOUGH DOGS?
AND NOW, RIN TIN CAN, ENOUGH JOKING AROUND! DO YOUR JOB, FOR ONCE!
WHAT... WHAT!?... I DON'T PULL!
WHAT'S THEIR PROBLEM?...
GRRRR
GRRR
THEY'RE FOLLOWING ME!...
DOING A HORSE'S JOB WILL DO HIM SOME GOOD!...
MORRIS & GOSCINNY
39B

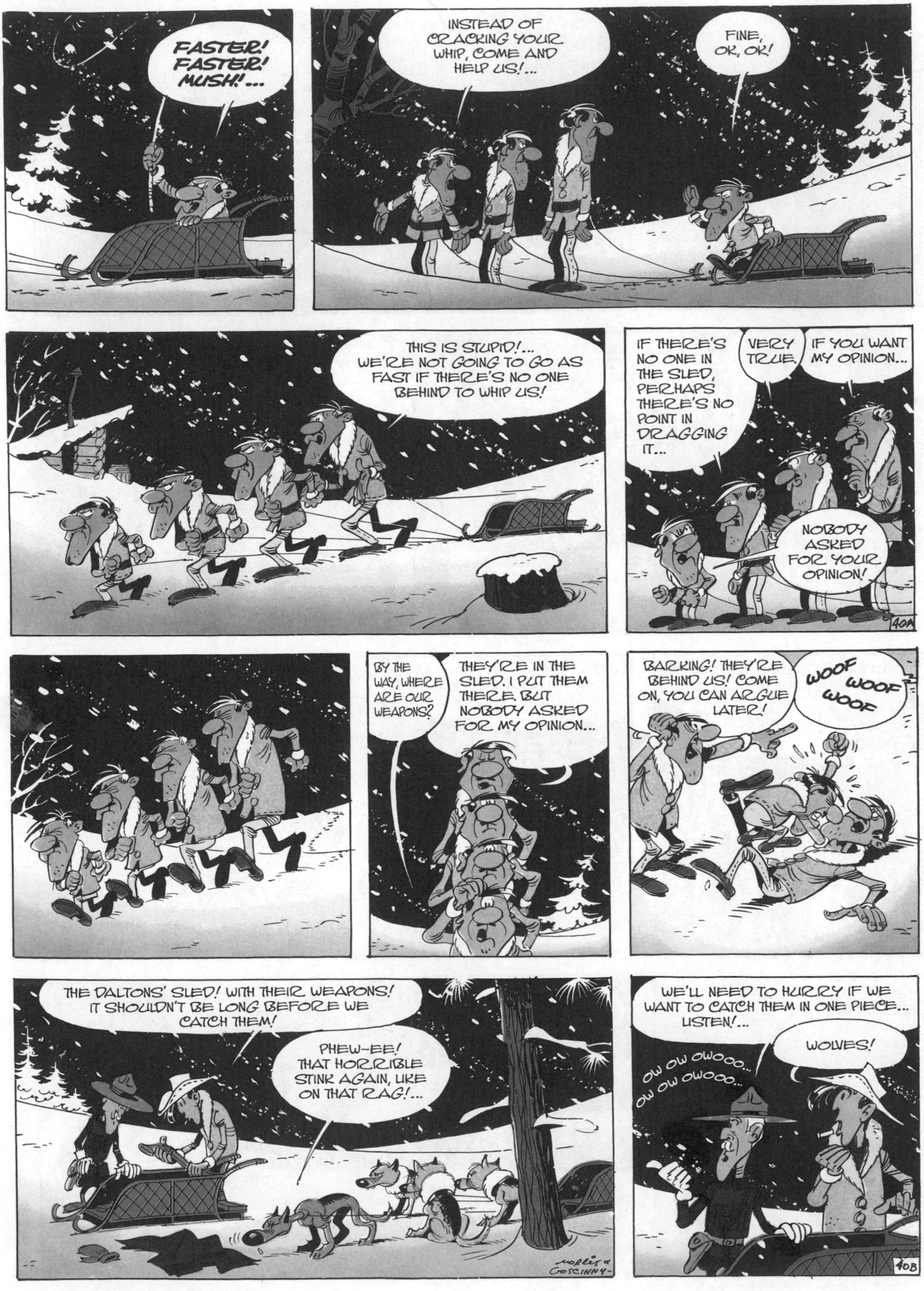
FASTER! FASTER! MUSH!...
INSTEAD OF CRACKING YOUR WHIP, COME AND HELP US!...
FINE, OK, OK!
THIS IS STUPID!... WE'RE NOT GOING TO GO AS FAST IF THERE'S NO ONE BEHIND TO WHIP US!
IF THERE'S NO ONE IN THE SLED, PERHAPS THERE'S NO POINT IN DRAGGING IT...
VERY TRUE.
IF YOU WANT MY OPINION...
NOBODY ASKED FOR YOUR OPINION!
40A
BY THE WAY, WHERE ARE OUR WEAPONS?
THEY'RE IN THE SLED. I PUT THEM THERE. BUT NOBODY ASKED FOR MY OPINION...
BARKING! THEY'RE BEHIND US! COME ON, YOU CAN ARGUE LATER!
WOOF WOOF WOOF
THE DALTONS' SLED! WITH THEIR WEAPONS! IT SHOULDN'T BE LONG BEFORE WE CATCH THEM!
PHEW-EE! THAT HORRIBLE STINK AGAIN, LIKE ON THAT RAG!...
MORRIS & GOSCINNY
WE'LL NEED TO HURRY IF WE WANT TO CATCH THEM IN ONE PIECE... LISTEN!...
OW OW OWOOO... OW OW OWOOO...
WOLVES!
40B

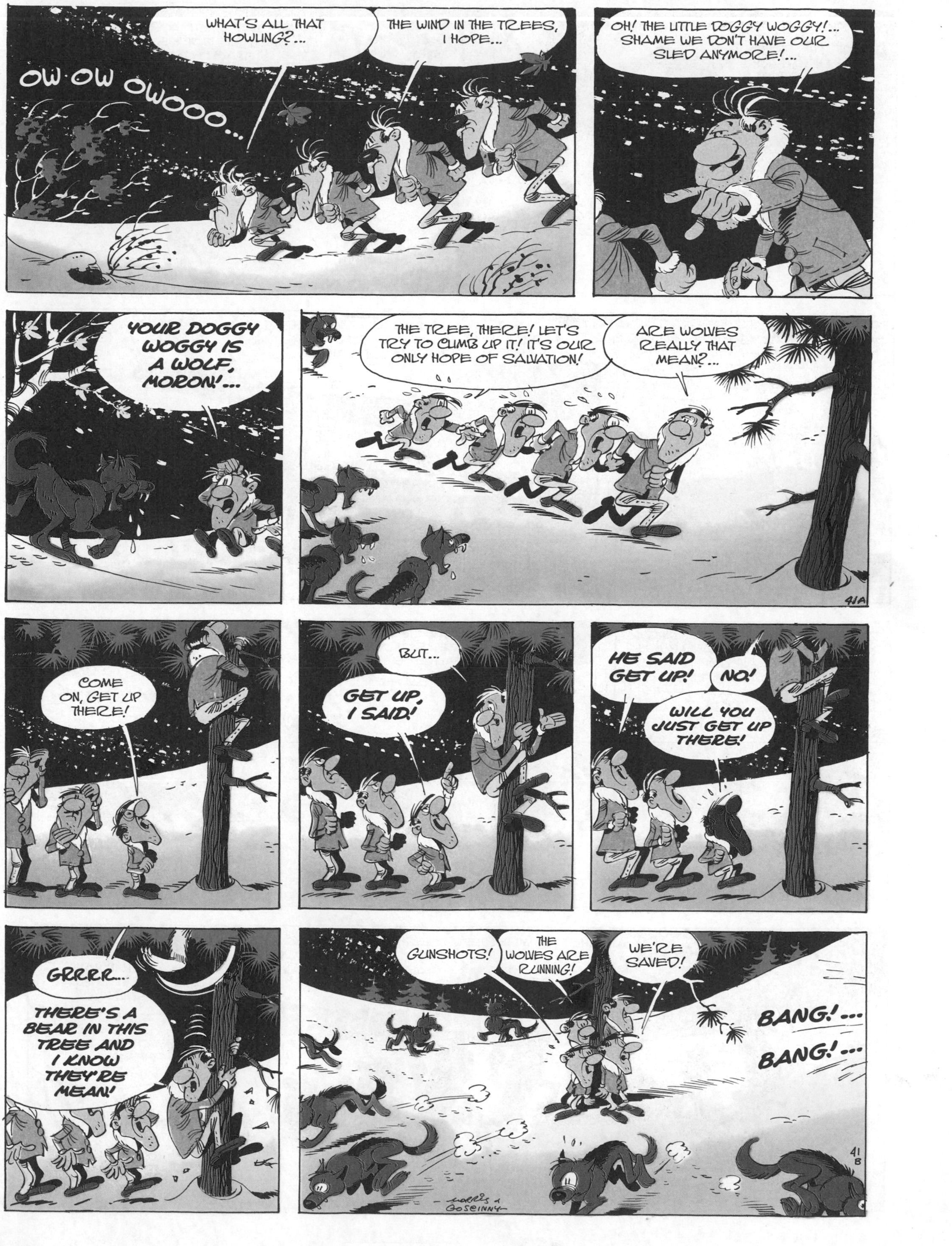

OW-OW OWOOO...
WHAT'S ALL THAT HOWLING?...
THE WIND IN THE TREES, I HOPE...
OH! THE LITTLE DOGGY WOGGY!... SHAME WE DON'T HAVE OUR SLED ANYMORE!...
YOUR DOGGY WOGGY IS A WOLF, MORON!...
THE TREE, THERE! LET'S TRY TO CLIMB UP IT! IT'S OUR ONLY HOPE OF SALVATION!
ARE WOLVES REALLY THAT MEAN?...
41A
COME ON, GET UP THERE!
BUT...
GET UP, I SAID!
HE SAID GET UP!
NO!
WILL YOU JUST GET UP THERE!
GRRRR...
THERE'S A BEAR IN THIS TREE AND I KNOW THEY'RE MEAN!
GUNSHOTS!
THE WOLVES ARE RUNNING!
WE'RE SAVED!
BANG!...
BANG!...
41 B
MORRIS & GOSCINNY

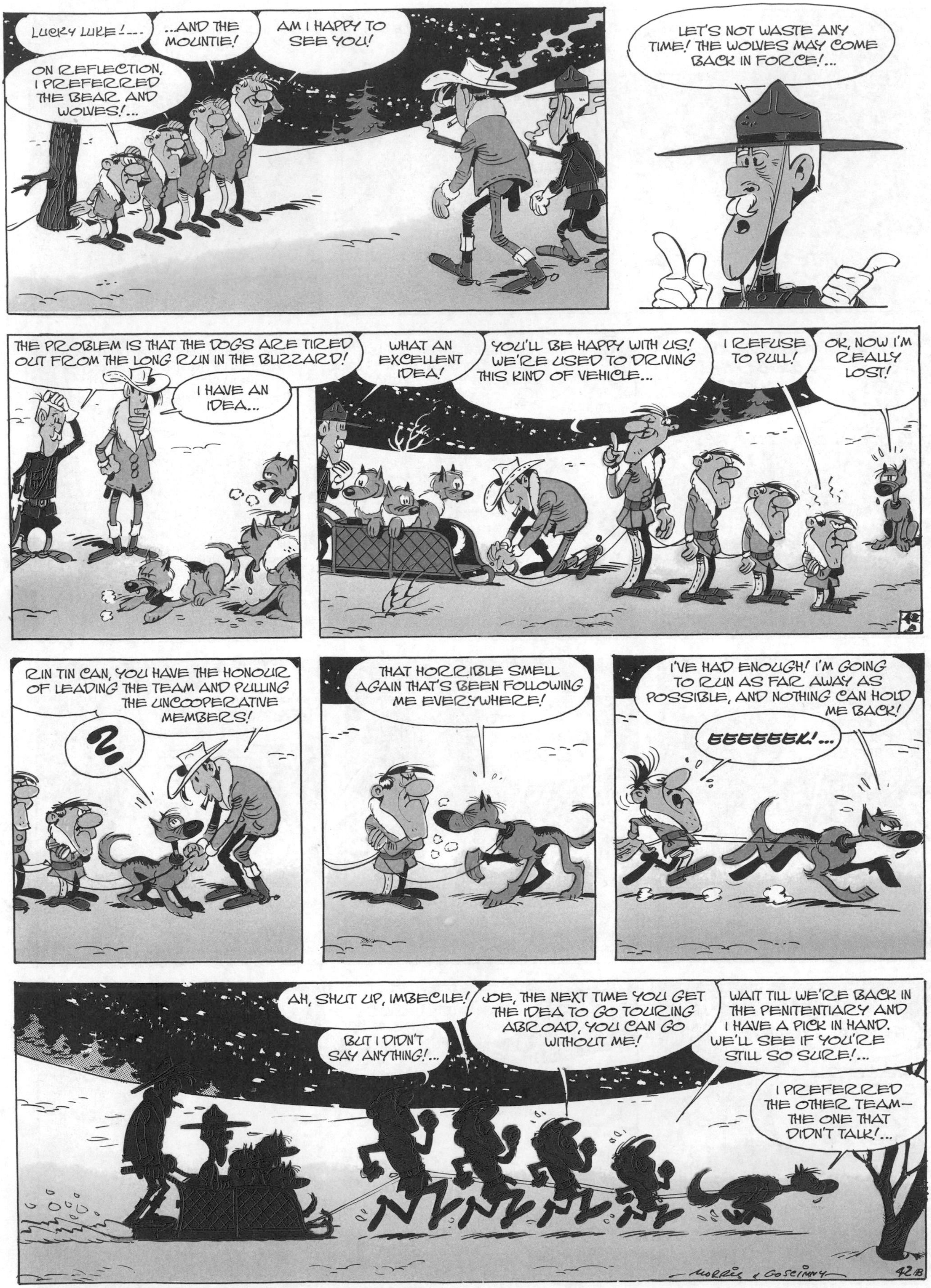
LUCKY LUKE!...
...AND THE MOUNTIE!
AM I HAPPY TO SEE YOU!
ON REFLECTION, I PREFERRED THE BEAR AND WOLVES!...
LET'S NOT WASTE ANY TIME! THE WOLVES MAY COME BACK IN FORCE!...
THE PROBLEM IS THAT THE DOGS ARE TIRED OUT FROM THE LONG RUN IN THE BLIZZARD!
I HAVE AN IDEA...
WHAT AN EXCELLENT IDEA!
YOU'LL BE HAPPY WITH US! WE'RE USED TO DRIVING THIS KIND OF VEHICLE...
I REFUSE TO PULL!
OK, NOW I'M REALLY LOST!
RIN TIN CAN, YOU HAVE THE HONOUR OF LEADING THE TEAM AND PULLING THE UNCOOPERATIVE MEMBERS!
?
THAT HORRIBLE SMELL AGAIN THAT'S BEEN FOLLOWING ME EVERYWHERE!
I'VE HAD ENOUGH! I'M GOING TO RUN AS FAR AWAY AS POSSIBLE, AND NOTHING CAN HOLD ME BACK!
EEEEEEK!...
AH, SHUT UP, IMBECILE!
BUT I DIDN'T SAY ANYTHING!...
JOE, THE NEXT TIME YOU GET THE IDEA TO GO TOURING ABROAD, YOU CAN GO WITHOUT ME!
WAIT TILL WE'RE BACK IN THE PENITENTIARY AND I HAVE A PICK IN HAND. WE'LL SEE IF YOU'RE STILL SO SURE!...
I PREFERRED THE OTHER TEAM— THE ONE THAT DIDN'T TALK!...
MORRIS & GOSCINNY
42B

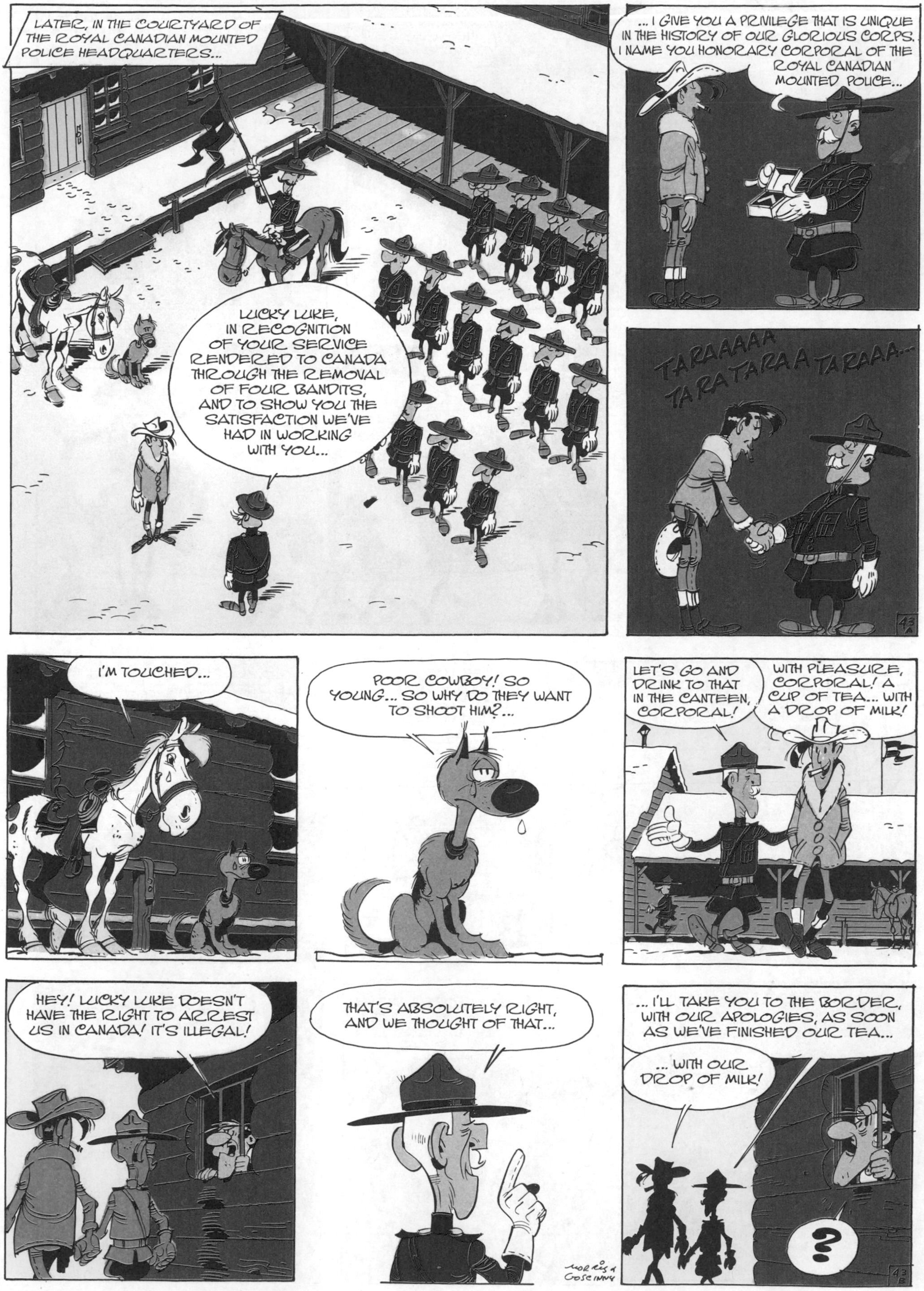
LATER, IN THE COURTYARD OF THE ROYAL CANADIAN MOUNTED POLICE HEADQUARTERS...
LUCKY LUKE, IN RECOGNITION OF YOUR SERVICE RENDERED TO CANADA THROUGH THE REMOVAL OF FOUR BANDITS, AND TO SHOW YOU THE SATISFACTION WE'VE HAD IN WORKING WITH YOU...
... I GIVE YOU A PRIVILEGE THAT IS UNIQUE IN THE HISTORY OF OUR GLORIOUS CORPS. I NAME YOU HONORARY CORPORAL OF THE ROYAL CANADIAN MOUNTED POLICE...
TARAAAAA TARATARAA TARAAA...
I'M TOUCHED...
POOR COWBOY! SO YOUNG... SO WHY DO THEY WANT TO SHOOT HIM?...
LET'S GO AND DRINK TO THAT IN THE CANTEEN, CORPORAL!
WITH PLEASURE, CORPORAL! A CUP OF TEA... WITH A DROP OF MILK!
HEY! LUCKY LUKE DOESN'T HAVE THE RIGHT TO ARREST US IN CANADA! IT'S ILLEGAL!
THAT'S ABSOLUTELY RIGHT, AND WE THOUGHT OF THAT...
... I'LL TAKE YOU TO THE BORDER, WITH OUR APOLOGIES, AS SOON AS WE'VE FINISHED OUR TEA...
... WITH OUR DROP OF MILK!
?
MORRIS & GOSCINNY

HERE WE ARE AT THE BORDER...
I'M HAPPY THAT THEY DECIDED TO HAVE MERCY ON THIS POOR COWBOY...
ADIOS, CORPORAL WINSTON PENDERGAST!
SEE YOU SOON, LUCKY LUKE!
AS FOR YOU, DALTONS, CANADA WILL NOT ARREST YOU: IT'S HAPPY JUST TO DEPORT YOU...
CANADA HOPES THAT YOU'LL HAVE GOOD MEMORIES OF YOUR TRIP...
ALL THE SAME, IT'S NICE TO BE HOME AGAIN.
IT WAS REALLY WORTH GOING ALL THAT WAY!
WELCOME TO THE UNITED STATES!
A FEW DAYS LATER...
HEY, BOYS! LUCKY LUKE AND THE DALTONS ARE BACK, AS EXPECTED!...
TRY TO KEEP THEM AT LEAST UNTIL THE NEW YEAR...
OH, DON'T YOU WORRY! THE DALTONS WON'T ESCAPE AGAIN. THEY'RE WELL GUARDED!
THAT'S IT! THAT'S IT! I CAN SIT!!
SEE FOR YOURSELF...
WELL, I DON'T THINK I'VE SEEN THE LAST OF THE DALTONS!!
♫... I'M A POOR LONESOME COWBOY... ♪
THE END
MORRIS & GOSCINNY

LUCKY LUKE

The man who shoots faster than his own shadow

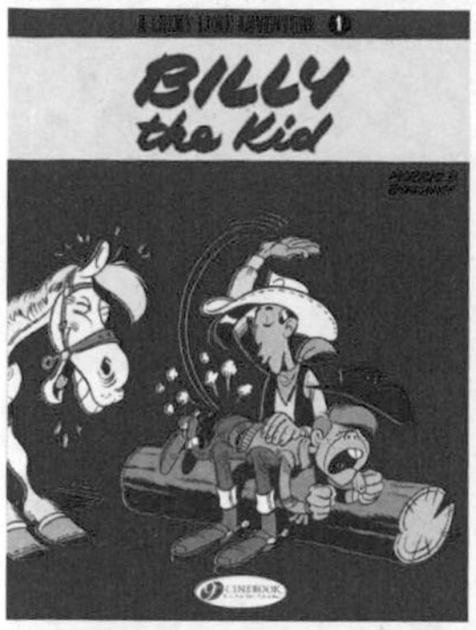
A LUCKY LUKE ADVENTURE 1
BILLY the Kid

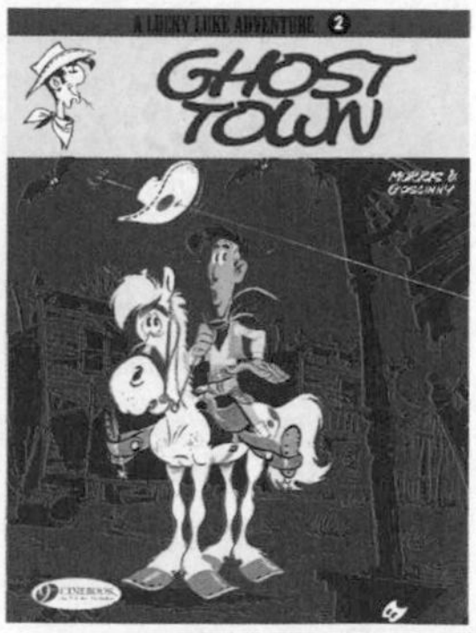
A LUCKY LUKE ADVENTURE 2
GHOST TOWN

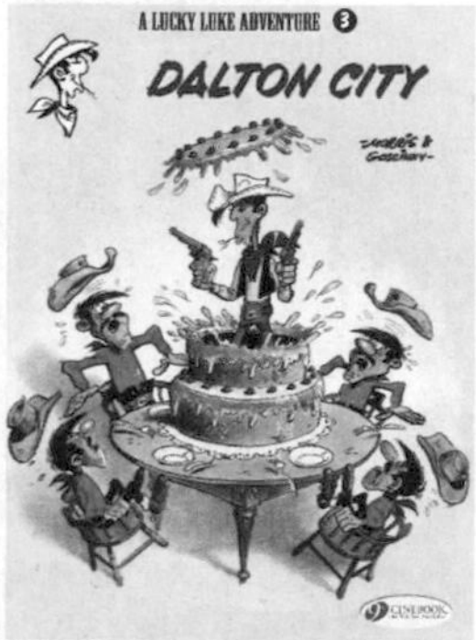
A LUCKY LUKE ADVENTURE 3
DALTON CITY

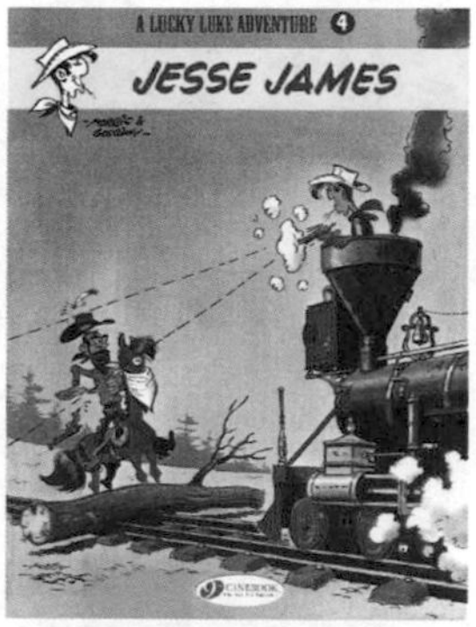
A LUCKY LUKE ADVENTURE 4
JESSE JAMES

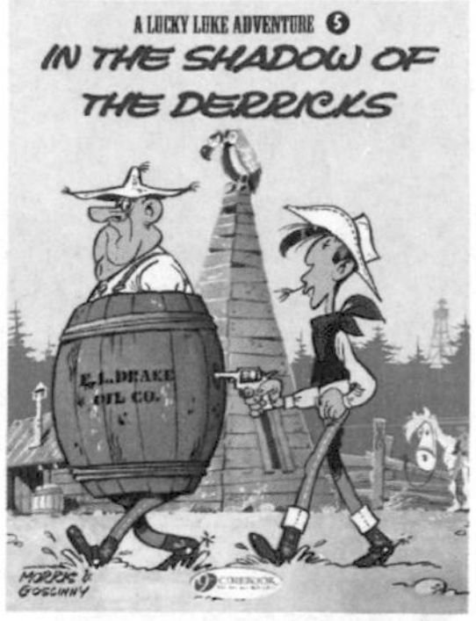
A LUCKY LUKE ADVENTURE 5
IN THE SHADOW OF THE DERRICKS
E.L. DRAKE OIL CO.

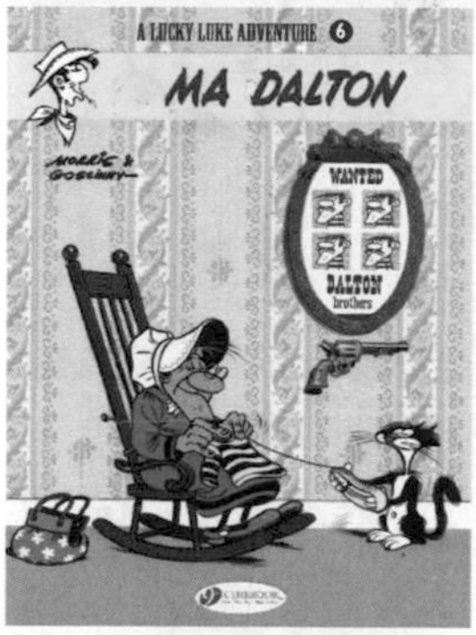
A LUCKY LUKE ADVENTURE 6
MA DALTON
WANTED
DALTON brothers

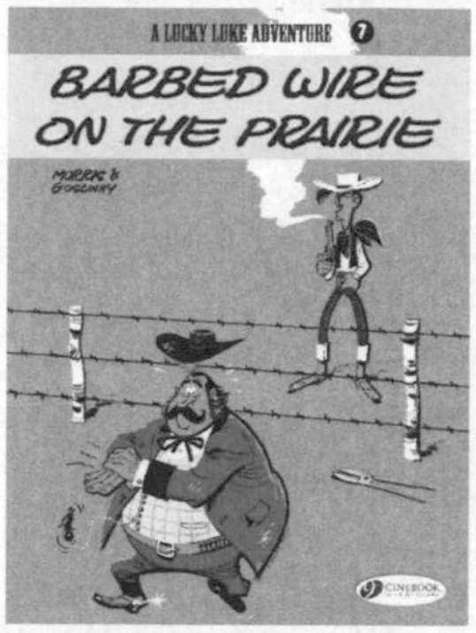
A LUCKY LUKE ADVENTURE 7
BARBED WIRE ON THE PRAIRIE

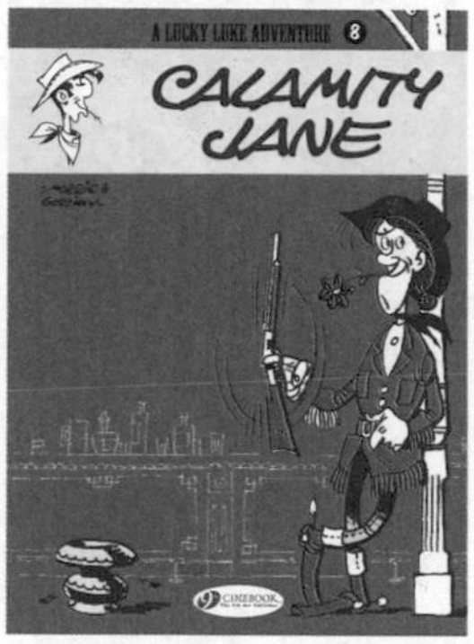
A LUCKY LUKE ADVENTURE 8
CALAMITY JANE

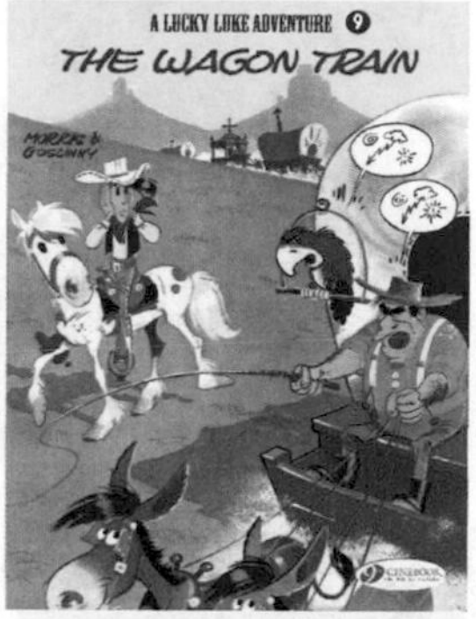
A LUCKY LUKE ADVENTURE 9
THE WAGON TRAIN

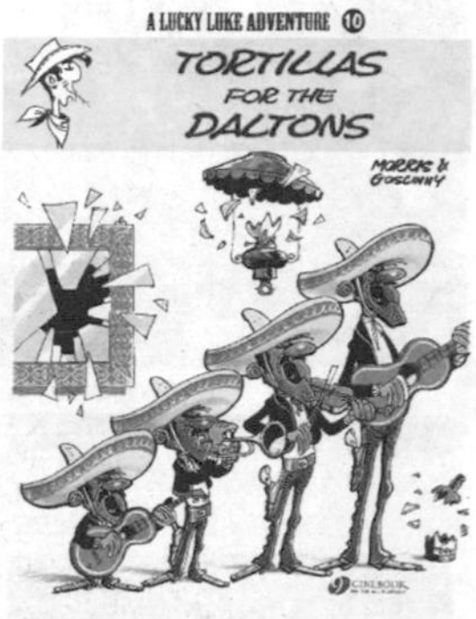
A LUCKY LUKE ADVENTURE 10
TORTILLAS FOR THE DALTONS

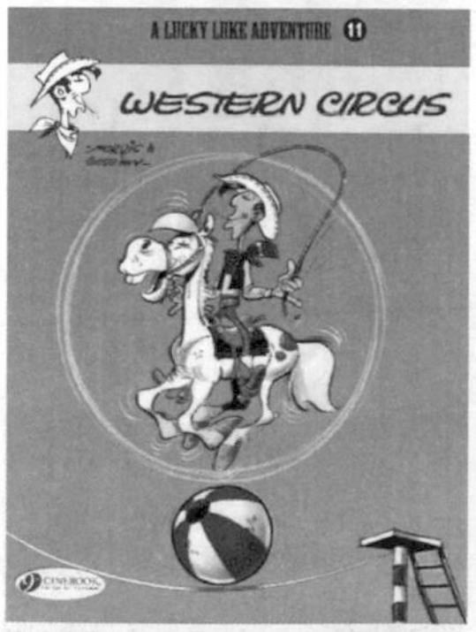
A LUCKY LUKE ADVENTURE 11
WESTERN CIRCUS

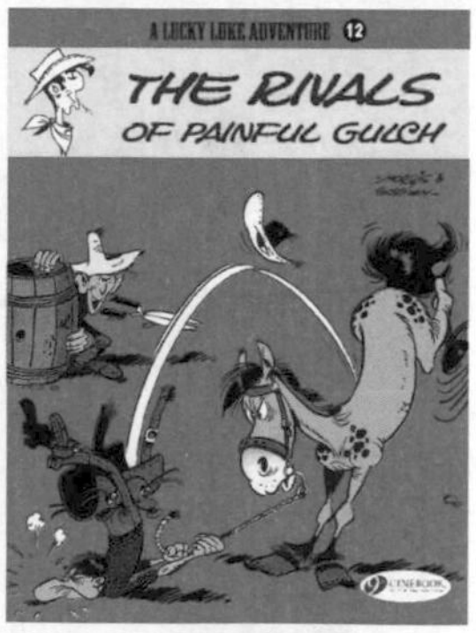
A LUCKY LUKE ADVENTURE 12
THE RIVALS OF PAINFUL GULCH

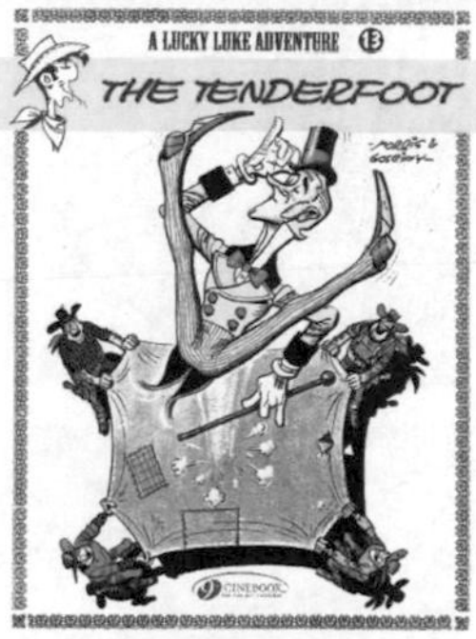
A LUCKY LUKE ADVENTURE 13
THE TENDERFOOT

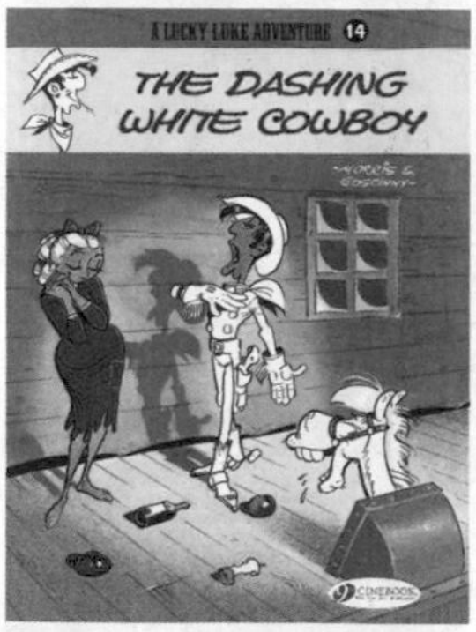
A LUCKY LUKE ADVENTURE 14
THE DASHING WHITE COWBOY

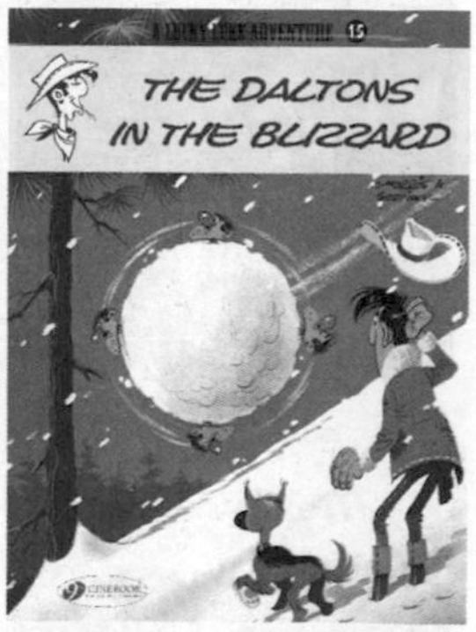
A LUCKY LUKE ADVENTURE 15
THE DALTONS IN THE BLIZZARD

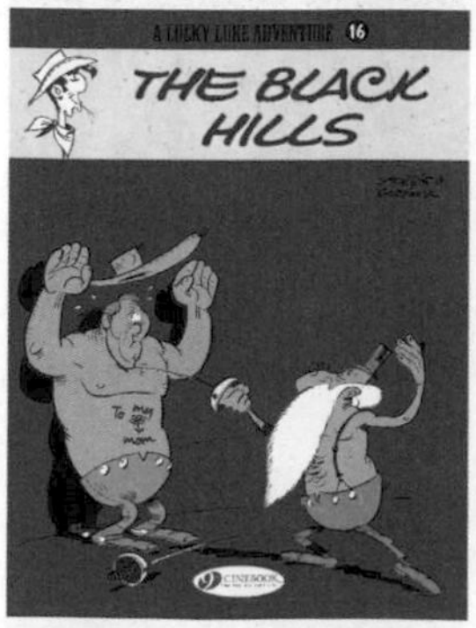
A LUCKY LUKE ADVENTURE 16
THE BLACK HILLS

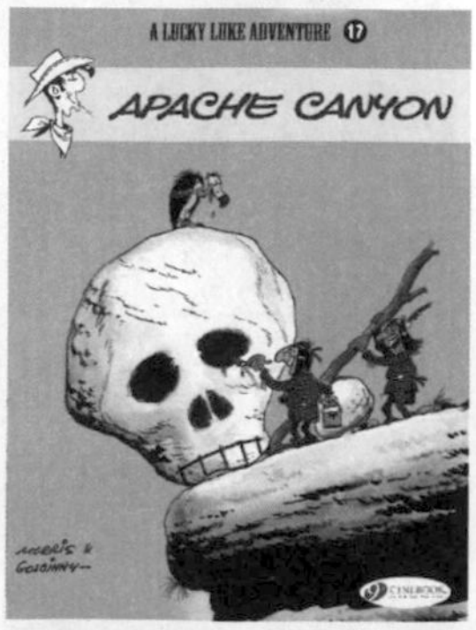
A LUCKY LUKE ADVENTURE 17
APACHE CANYON

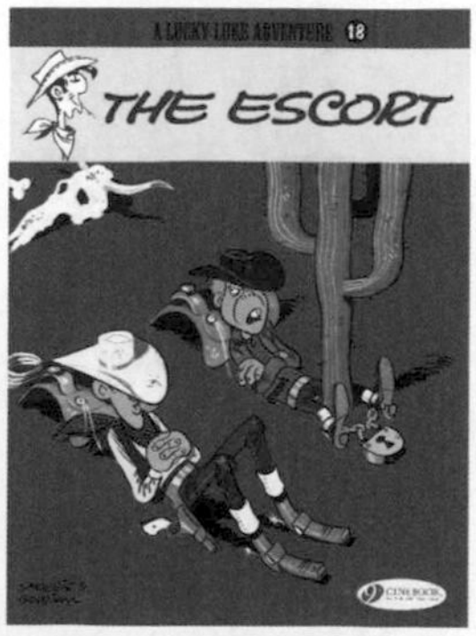
A LUCKY LUKE ADVENTURE 18
THE ESCORT

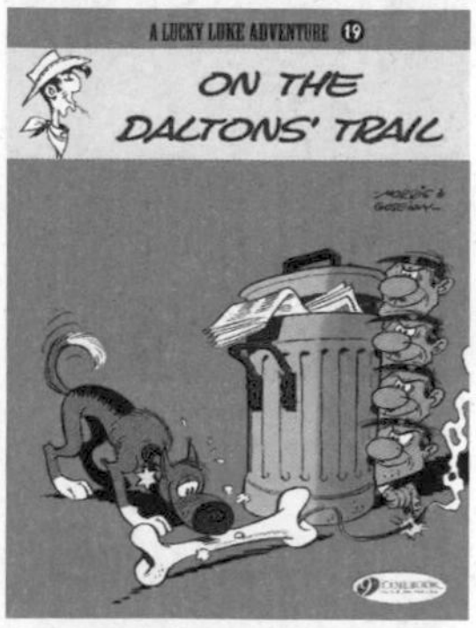
A LUCKY LUKE ADVENTURE 19
ON THE DALTONS' TRAIL

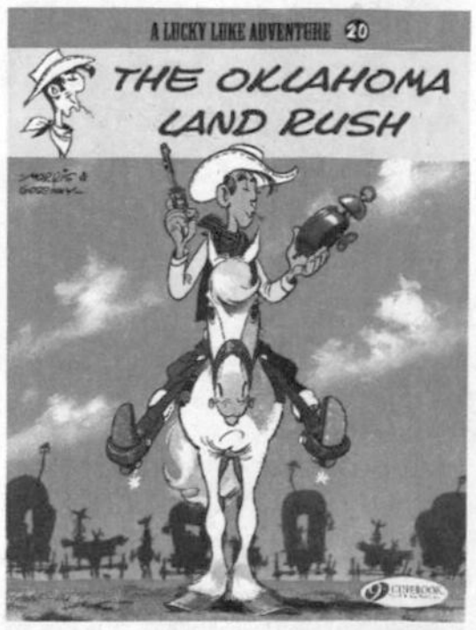
A LUCKY LUKE ADVENTURE 20
THE OKLAHOMA LAND RUSH

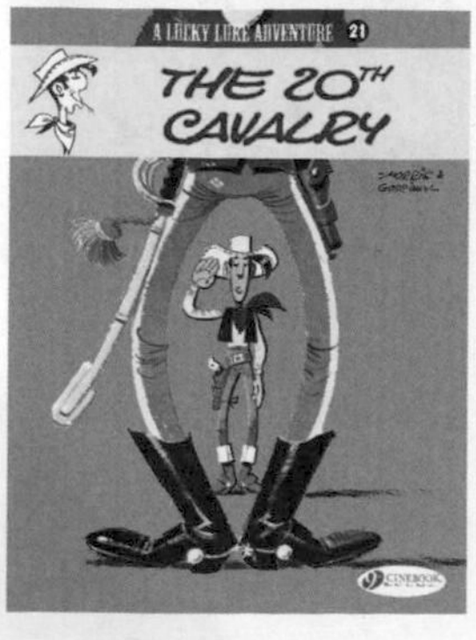
A LUCKY LUKE ADVENTURE 21
THE 20TH CAVALRY

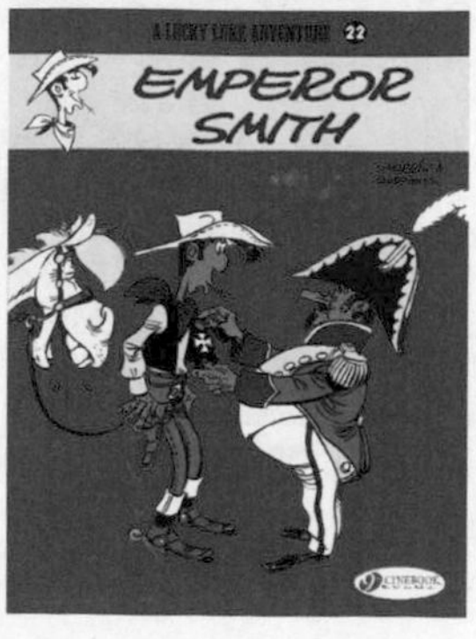
A LUCKY LUKE ADVENTURE 22
EMPEROR SMITH

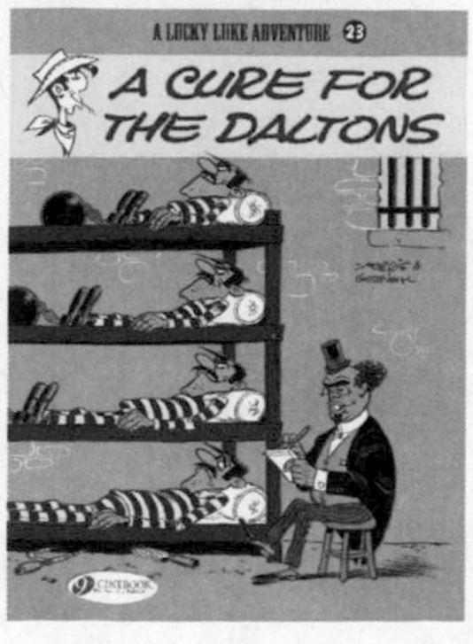
A LUCKY LUKE ADVENTURE 23
A CURE FOR THE DALTONS

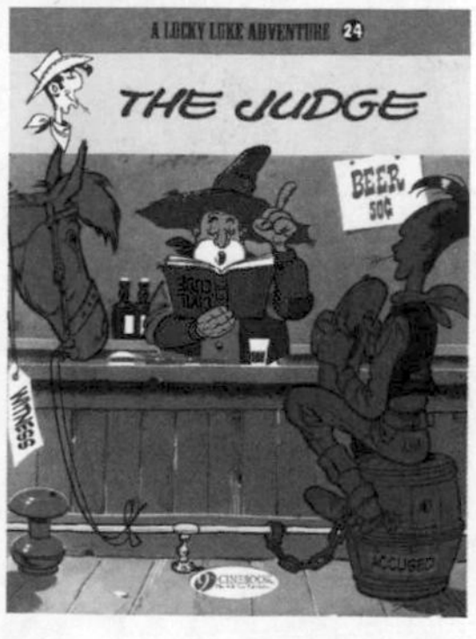
A LUCKY LUKE ADVENTURE 24
THE JUDGE
BEER

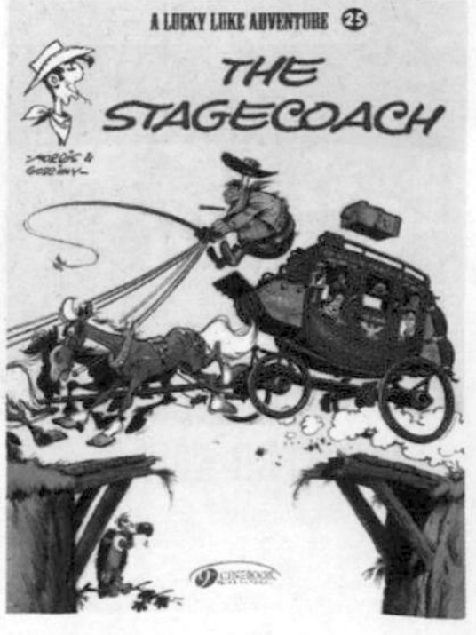
A LUCKY LUKE ADVENTURE 25
THE STAGECOACH

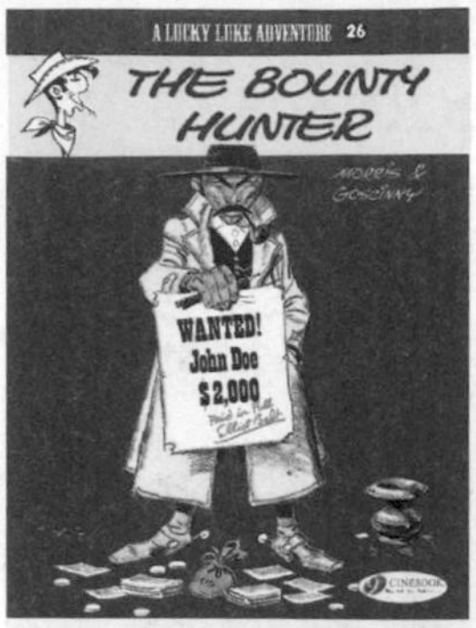
A LUCKY LUKE ADVENTURE 26
THE BOUNTY HUNTER
WANTED! John Doe $2,000

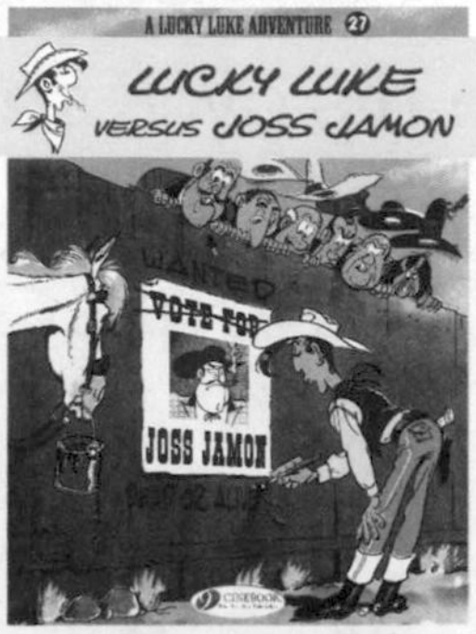
A LUCKY LUKE ADVENTURE 27
LUCKY LUKE VERSUS JOSS JAMON
VOTE FOR
JOSS JAMON

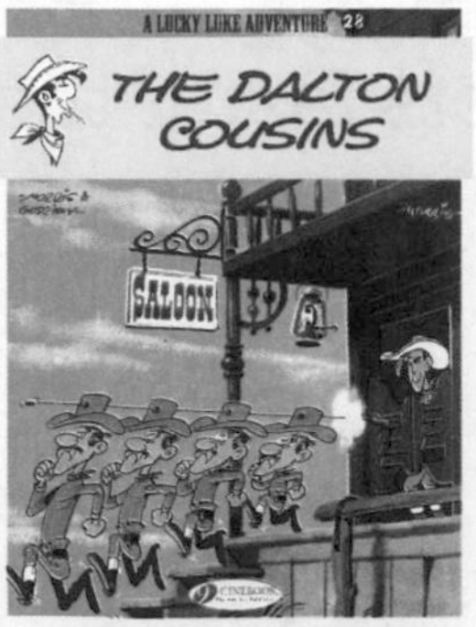
A LUCKY LUKE ADVENTURE 28
THE DALTON COUSINS
SALOON

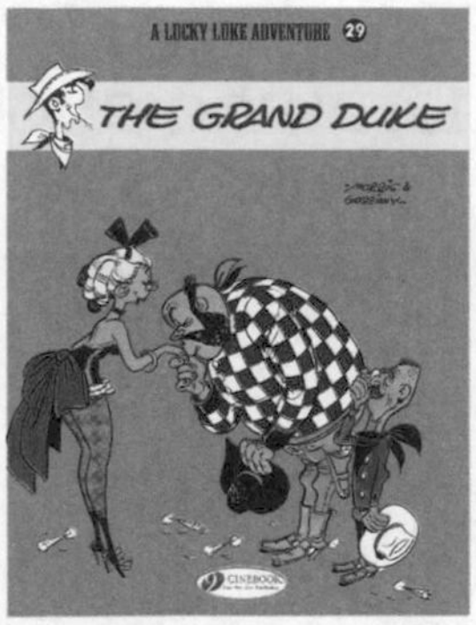
A LUCKY LUKE ADVENTURE 29
THE GRAND DUKE

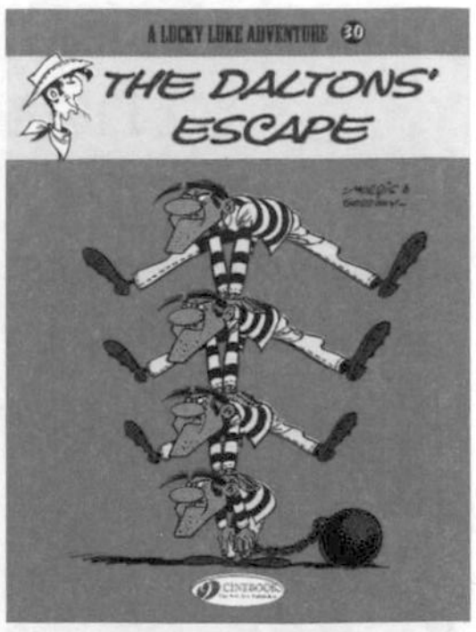
A LUCKY LUKE ADVENTURE 30
THE DALTONS' ESCAPE

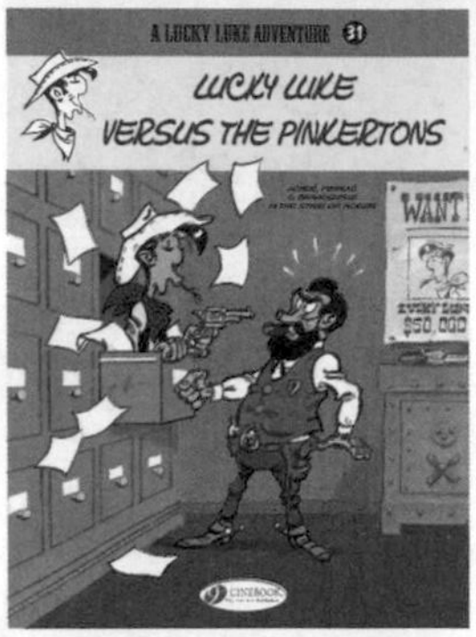
A LUCKY LUKE ADVENTURE 31
LUCKY LUKE VERSUS THE PINKERTONS

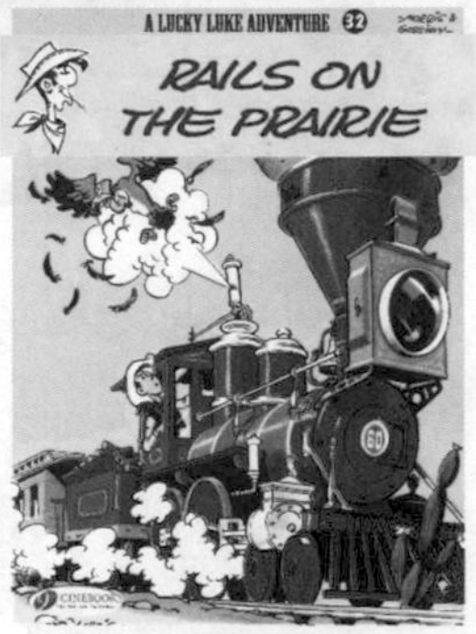
A LUCKY LUKE ADVENTURE 32
RAILS ON THE PRAIRIE

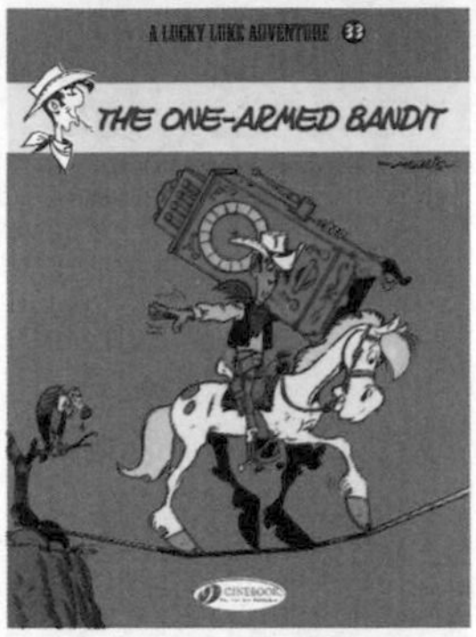
A LUCKY LUKE ADVENTURE 33
THE ONE-ARMED BANDIT

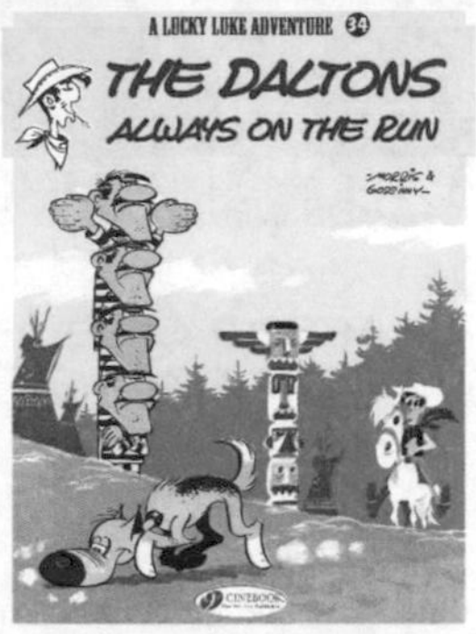
A LUCKY LUKE ADVENTURE 34
THE DALTONS ALWAYS ON THE RUN

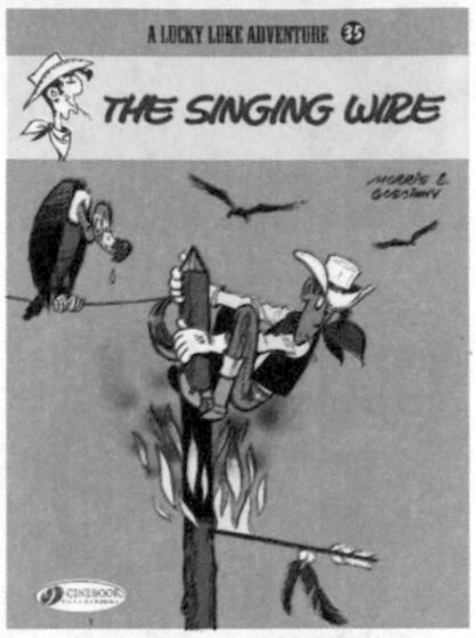
A LUCKY LUKE ADVENTURE 35
THE SINGING WIRE

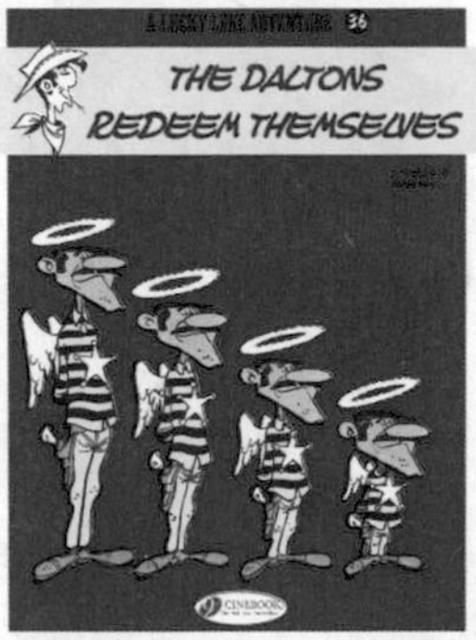
A LUCKY LUKE ADVENTURE 36
THE DALTONS REDEEM THEMSELVES

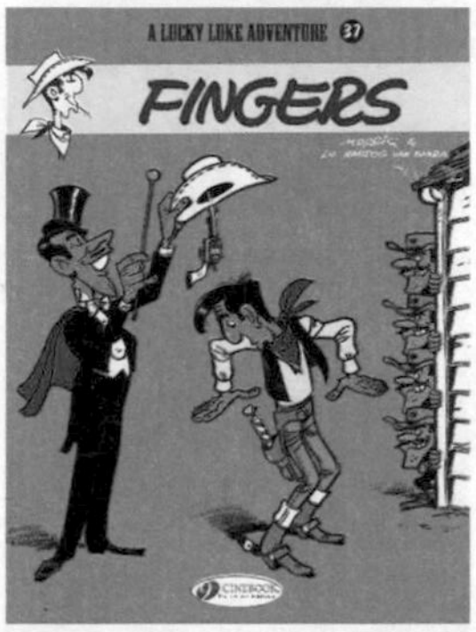
A LUCKY LUKE ADVENTURE 37
FINGERS

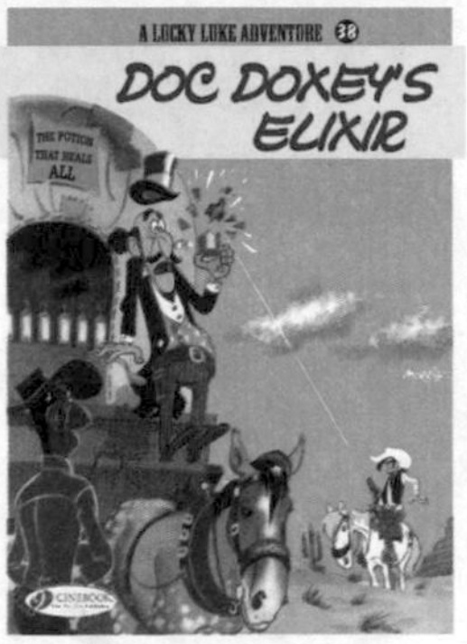
A LUCKY LUKE ADVENTURE 38
DOC DOXEY'S ELIXIR

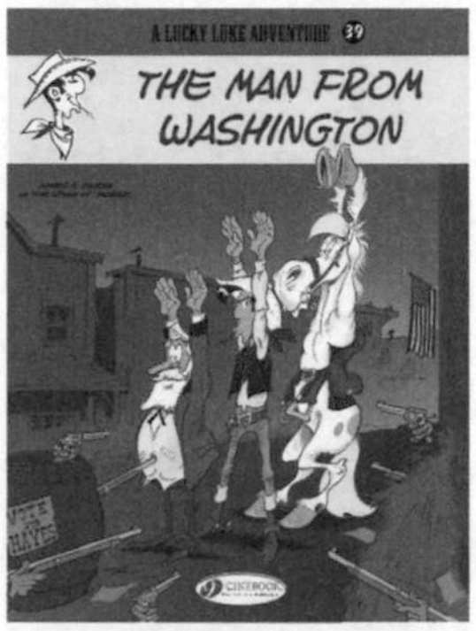
A LUCKY LUKE ADVENTURE 39
THE MAN FROM WASHINGTON

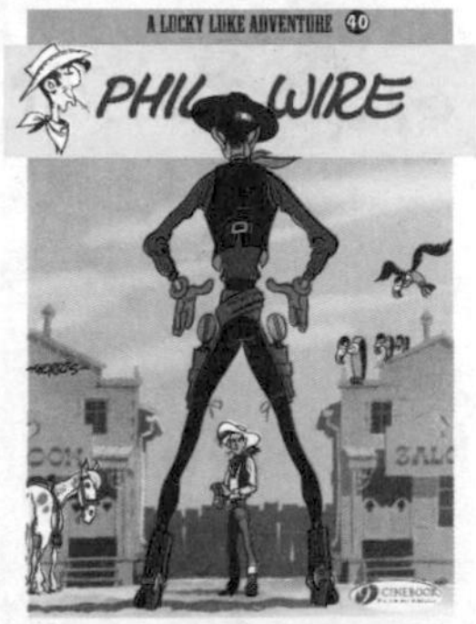
A LUCKY LUKE ADVENTURE 40
PHIL WIRE

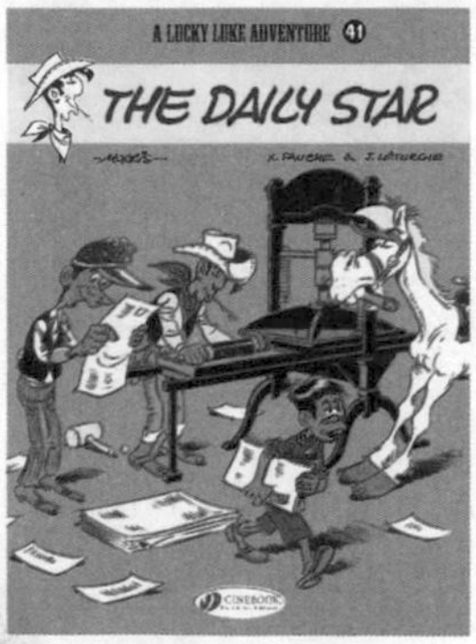
A LUCKY LUKE ADVENTURE 41
THE DAILY STAR

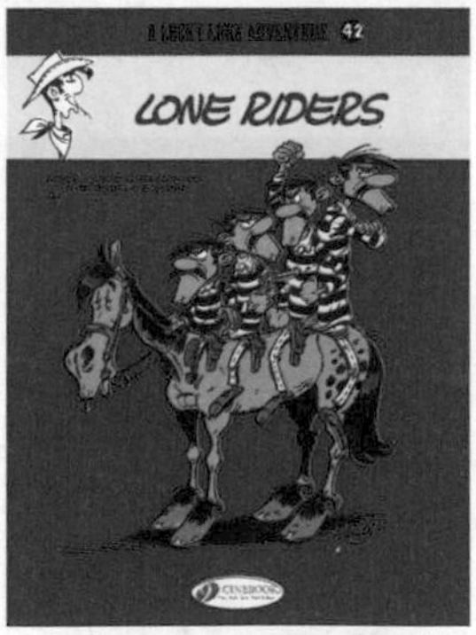
A LUCKY LUKE ADVENTURE 42
LONE RIDERS

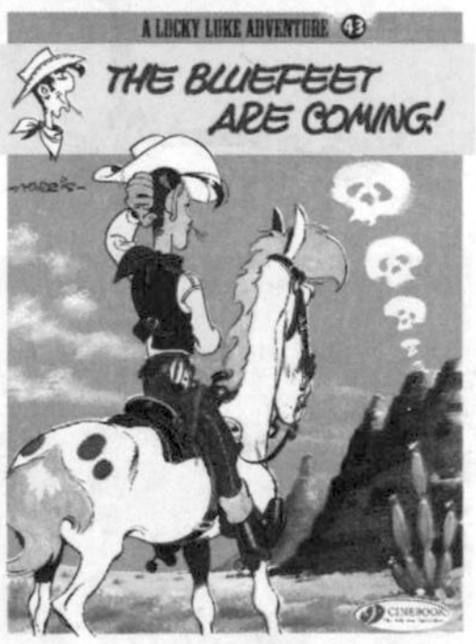
A LUCKY LUKE ADVENTURE 43
THE BLUEFEET ARE COMING!

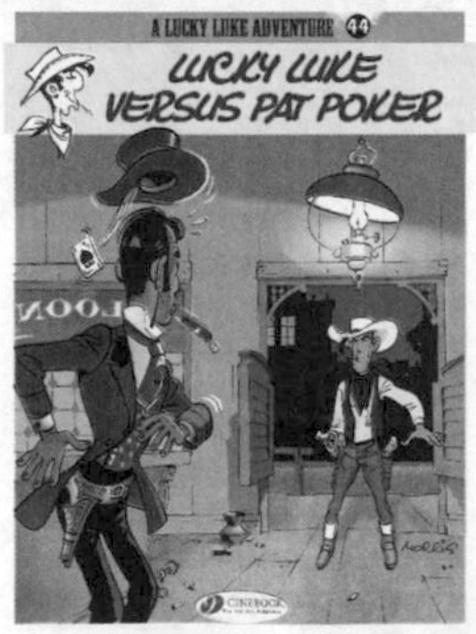
A LUCKY LUKE ADVENTURE 44
LUCKY LUKE VERSUS PAT POKER

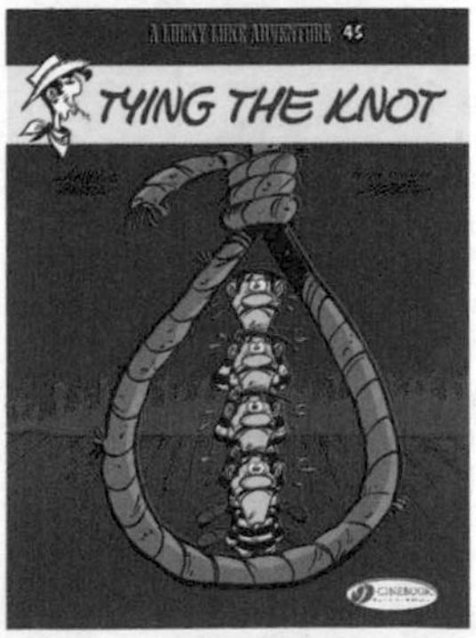
A LUCKY LUKE ADVENTURE 45
TYING THE KNOT

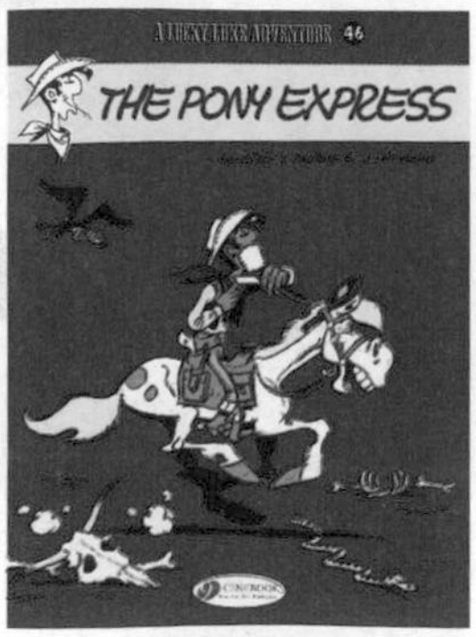
A LUCKY LUKE ADVENTURE 46
THE PONY EXPRESS

APRIL 2014

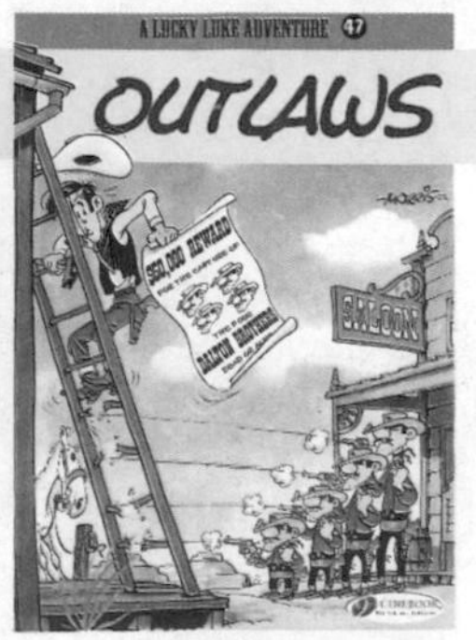
A LUCKY LUKE ADVENTURE 47
OUTLAWS
SALOON

JUNE 2014

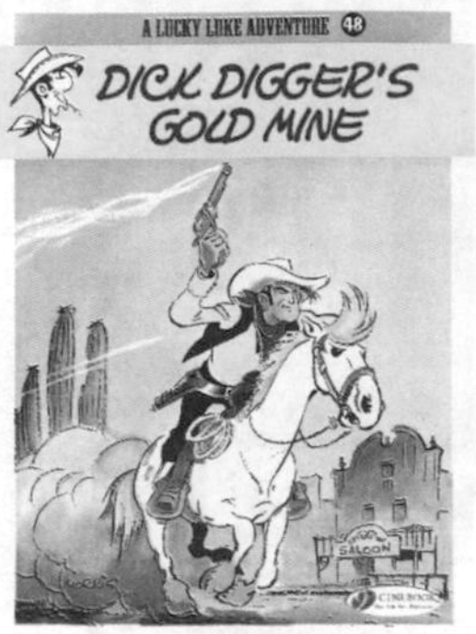
A LUCKY LUKE ADVENTURE 48
DICK DIGGER'S GOLD MINE

AUGUST 2014

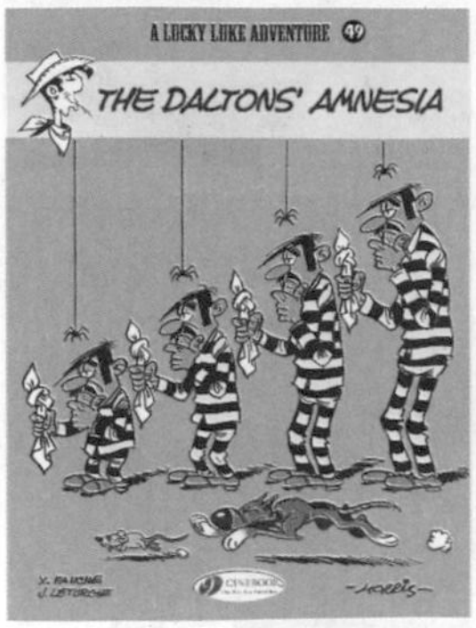
A LUCKY LUKE ADVENTURE 49
THE DALTONS' AMNESIA

OCTOBER 2014

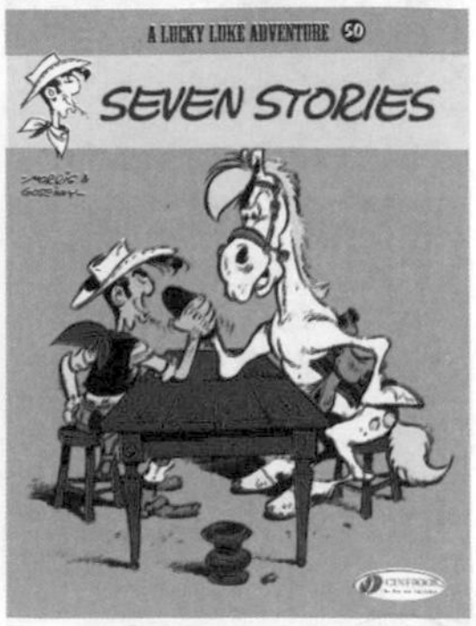
A LUCKY LUKE ADVENTURE 50
SEVEN STORIES

DECEMBER 2014